Riding the Line

The flare-up between Zeb Walters of the Red Hammer ranch and Broken Arrow's top-hand, Jim Braddock, is brief and unexpected. It earns Zeb a lump on the head, a night in the cells and a five dollar fine. The cause is a mystery to everyone, including Jim Braddock, but over the following days, the event becomes a major talking point in Big Timber, giving rise to much gossip and speculation.

It is several weeks, however, before Jim and Zeb meet again, this time on the snow-swept bank of a creek that forms the boundary between the two ranches. The outcome leads to death and violence, lost trust, a new ally, the threat of range war and a noose around Jim Braddock's neck.

Riding the Line

Will DuRey

A Black Horse Western

ROBERT HALE

© Will DuRey 2017
First published in Great Britain 2017

ISBN 978-0-7198-2153-0

The Crowood Press
The Stable Block
Crowood Lane
Ramsbury
Marlborough
Wiltshire SN8 2HR

www.bhwesterns.com

Robert Hale is an imprint
of The Crowood Press

The right of Will DuRey to be identified as
author of this work has been asserted by him
in accordance with the Copyright, Designs and
Patents Act 1988

Typeset by
Derek Doyle & Associates, Shaw Heath
Printed and bound in Great Britain by
CPI Group (UK) Ltd, Croydon, CR0 4YY

PROLOGUE

Nobody really knew the cause of the flare-up in The Garter, not even Jim Braddock, who was a major player in the incident. It was two days after payday and, in keeping with custom, riders from the Broken Arrow spread had ridden into Big Timber at the earliest opportunity to sample the entertainment on offer. That boiled down to whiskey, a nickel-and-dime card game in one of the saloons and the company of one of their girls for an hour. More wranglers and drovers who were flush with their month-end dollar-a-day pay from the other outfits in the vicinity were also in town, their needs no different from those of the hardworking Broken Arrow crew.

Zeb Walters had a wife and daughter, so when he drifted into The Garter among the Red Hammer cowboys it wasn't to flip a dollar to one of the girls and make use of one of the rooms along the upstairs balcony. He'd worked on Charlie Grisham's spread for eight years and was reckoned to be one of the smarter fellows who pushed cows for a living. With a family in tow when he arrived in Big Timber, folk had expected him to work his own strip but nothing had come of that. Eight years on he was still working another man's cattle. After buying a beer he looked around the room, then pulled out a chair at one of the tables where a poker game was in progress. He knew all the people gathered there: two men who lived in Big Timber, a wrangler from a small ranch south of town and Jim Braddock from the Broken Arrow.

Compared to the big money games that were common in the cities, rich cow towns and mining camps, they were playing for pennies, but these were men cautious with their money, anxious to make it last until the next payday. However, Lady Luck had chosen that day to drape herself around Jim Braddock and hadn't released him. As the hours passed more than one player remarked upon his formidable good fortune and quit the table to find a game in another part of The Garter or a saloon elsewhere in town. Zeb Walters had not quit, insisting that his luck must eventually change. It hadn't, and exchanging cold beer for shots of rotgut whiskey didn't improve matters either. He became more angry and more drunk with each losing hand.

Jim Braddock and Zeb Walters weren't friends but neither were they enemies. They'd known each other for several years but past hostilities between the men who paid them had prevented any real friendships from being formed between riders of the opposing outfits. Still, Jim didn't want to take all of the other cowboy's pay; he had had his own bleak periods of seeking handouts from his bunkhouse cronies when he'd done foolish things. It would be worse for Zeb with a family to support, but the decision to keep playing wasn't Jim's to make. It was accepted practice to play on if the other man was determined to try to win his money back. Zeb had ignored the counsel of one or two friends during the session, had refused to leave the game.

Low murmured curses and the occasional blazing-eyed look across the table at Jim had made everyone aware of Zeb's growing belligerence, but they weren't unaccustomed to that. Zeb often grumbled, often conveyed the impression that the fates had conspired to make every event in his life a failure, but it never developed into anger, he had no reputation for violent behaviour. So his sudden awkward lurch to his feet as Jim reached across the table to scoop up the pot that contained the last of Zeb's money came as a surprise. The clumsiness of his abrupt movement caused his chair to overturn and topple to the floor and it was its clatter that gripped the attention of everyone in the room. All eyes turned in that direction, watched as Zeb hunched his shoulders, his right hand hovering close to the butt of his holstered gun. He extended his left hand in accusatory fashion, his mouth was open, saliva dribbling from the corner and words were forming in his mind but were unable to find

7

their way to his mouth. Everyone knew he was dangerously close to calling Jim Braddock a cheat.

Jim Braddock was no more a gunfighter than Zeb Walters, but that day, with the other man unsteady with drink, the Broken Arrow rider would have had little trouble in beating his opponent to the draw. Throughout his life he'd seen men die; from the war years, through cattle drives and rough railhead towns, to warding off rustlers and riding with justly formed posses in pursuit of killers and robbers. He wasn't a man who enjoyed killing but nor was he one to avoid it if it was the right thing to do. He'd won twenty-two dollars from Zeb Walters that day, which, in his opinion, wasn't worth dying for, but if Zeb had reached for his gun Jim would have killed him. That was the way such matters were settled, but the long barrel of Sheriff Stone's Colt struck Zeb Walters on the side of the head and the Red Hammer rider slumped unconscious to the floor.

ONE

It wasn't dawn; perhaps it would be another hour before sufficient light penetrated the interior of the small line shack to enable Jim Braddock to find his boots, fill the coffee pot and see his breath hovering in the air. It was the cold that had awoken him; had, in fact, kept him on the edge of wakefulness throughout the night despite being wrapped in the new grey blanket he'd brought from the bunkhouse stores. If he hadn't been under orders to be tough on Dean Ridgeway he wouldn't have endured the torment. He would have supplemented the warmth provided by the blanket by heaping his big coat over it, thereby ensuring a good night's sleep, but he'd made some bravado statements about it not yet being winter, with the result that he would have lost face if he'd taken steps to relieve his suffering. So he'd persevered in silence. Although he'd expected a colder night, its severity had caught him by surprise. In hindsight, he should have packed the stove with logs to keep it alive and let its heat ward off the night chills, but he hadn't and he'd had to face up to the consequences; lacking a good night's sleep meant the day ahead would be all the more arduous.

Across the room, where he lay on a rolled-out mattress, Dean Ridgeway cursed, using an expression that not only spoke of his gross discomfort but also included imprecations wishing evil upon his father and Jim, both of whom he blamed for his current plight. The bitter words were uttered no louder than the laboured, teeth-chattering exhalations of breath with which they were intermingled but Jim had heard them throughout the night, at first with humour, then with a level of sympathy and now with a degree of annoyance.

'I don't care if you are the boss's son,' he snarled, 'but if you call me that name again I'll beat you stupid, tie you across your saddle and send you back down to the ranch.'

'You're awake!'

'Of course I'm awake. Who can sleep with you yammering like an underpaid gal in Miss Lily's house.'

'Wish I was there now,' Dean grumbled, 'being warmed by Rosie.'

'What!' exclaimed Jim, 'are you cold? Well put some clothes on and light the stove.'

Defensively, Dean repudiated Jim's suggestion. 'I didn't say I was cold.'

In the darkness the older man grinned. 'Well,' he

10

said in a grumbling tone, 'you've spoilt my sleep so we might as well have some coffee.'

After lighting the stub of candle that remained in the holder on the small table, Jim dressed hurriedly and wondered at the logic behind the old man's efforts to produce a mirror-image of himself in his son. He understood, of course, that the Broken Arrow was Hec Ridgeway's life's work and his legacy for future generations. A man like Hec who had built his own little empire would hope for, expect – *want* – his son to follow in his footsteps and build upon that inheritance, but it was clear to every man who rode for the Broken Arrow that young Dean wasn't cut out to be the hard-riding, knock-'em-down kind of rancher that was the mark of his father.

That wasn't to say there was no good in the lad, nor that he wouldn't amount to something if left to choose his own way in life. He was bright, intelligent and willing enough to do his share of work; he simply had no interest in cattle and no patience to learn about them or nurse them. If Hec had got the boy interested in the business aspects of ranching, breeding and profit making, Dean might have been an asset to his pa, but sending him out to chivvy dumb critters was more likely to drive him away than kindle any interest.

Cattle were dumb, Jim believed; sometimes they acted on instinct but never with intelligence. Herding them was a job for those who, like him, were capable of nothing better. Although he

11

didn't doubt that the old man had his son's best interests at heart, Jim was sure that treating Dean like a common drover was a waste of the lad's abilities.

The cabin wasn't large, it hadn't been built to accommodate more than one cowboy, so it wasn't easy for two big men to get dressed swiftly while stumbling about in the dimness of the confined space. By the time Jim was stamping his feet into his boots, however, Dean was making an effort to get the stove burning. When they'd eaten the eggs and ham prepared by Jim for breakfast, the dim, natural morning light assured them that their working day had begun.

Ice had formed overnight and sealed the door closed. It required a determined effort from Jim to crack it open. Outside, the sky above was clear but he could feel the stirring of a wind that was carrying the cold air from the Bitterroots. He looked westwards to their dark, ragged outline, turned up the collar of his heavy coat and crossed to the shed where the horses had been stabled. The hard ground was white with ice and frost. Once or twice his feet slipped as he trudged the distance between shack and shed. The warmth that escaped from the small stable when he opened the flimsy door was accompanied by the aroma of fresh manure. Jim was always comforted by the smell; his horse was alive and well, which was essential for his own survival, especially when line-riding at this remote extremity of the Broken Arrow range.

Dean, who had been banking the stove in an effort to keep it alight until they returned later in the day, joined Jim at the stable.

'What'll we do today?' he asked.

'Same as we do every day, round up strays and cut out Red Hammer stock.' As they led their horses out of the stable, Jim cast a look at the lightening sky. 'I don't like it,' he told his companion, directing his attention to the heavy, cloud-filled northern quarter. 'If this is the onset of winter it's going to be long and harsh. Wouldn't expect it to be this cold for another three weeks and if those clouds are full of snow we need to get the cattle out of the high ground straight away.'

'Perhaps it's just a squall,' suggested the younger man.

'You might be right, but let's get busy and be prepared for the worst.'

'Where are we going?'

'The highest they'll stray is the water hole up by the old Indian burial ground.'

'Why don't they go higher?'

'Nothing grows. They won't go where there isn't any grazing.'

'Smart of them to know that,' said Dean.

'Not smart,' Jim corrected, 'just instinct.'

Like a lot of cowboys employed by his father, Dean knew that Jim wasn't keen on long conversations. He had a tendency to be abrupt when he was running out of words, a trait that had regularly surfaced during the three weeks they'd been working the line together.

'That burial ground is up north apiece,' he said, hoping the snippet of knowledge would convince the older man that he had learned a lot under his tutelage. If Jim gave the old man a good report when they got back to the ranch he might never have to live in such primitive conditions again.

'That's right, but we'll check the eastern border first. Could be I'll need you to drive any strays we find over there back across to the Long Valley while I climb up to check the top water hole.' After a moment he spoke again. 'Is your rifle loaded?'

'Sure,' Dean assured him, the expression on his face a clear indication that he didn't understand the reason for the other's question.

'Wolves and lions,' Jim said. 'They'll be thinking of winter, too. If they can isolate one of the critters they'll attack it. Shoot to kill.'

'I know,' Dean replied, offended by the older man's implication that he wasn't tough enough to do what needed to be done to protect the stock.

'Kill as many as you can,' Jim told him. 'There's a bounty on wolf skins.'

'Cats, too?'

'Not a bounty but you'll be able to sell a good pelt at Morgan Taff's place in Big Timber. He'll give you a good price.'

As they rode away from the line cabin Dean Ridgeway mulled over Jim's words and questioned him about the value of pelts and their barter value in earlier days.

'Sure,' Jim assured him, 'when I first came to these parts it was the most common way of doing business. Paid for all my provisions and ammunition with wolf skins and other hides.'

'Were you a trapper?'

'No, but I learned to skin deer and beaver and anything else I killed. One time I traded a bearskin in a Shoshone village for a whole wardrobe of buckskin: shirt, leggings and moccasins, plus a few trinkets. Got a nice necklace that I used to pay for a girl in a Missoula sporting house.'

Dean laughed. 'Bartering in a place like Miss Lily's?'

'Sure,' Jim insisted. 'This girl had a neck two feet long to accommodate all the trinkets she'd earned.'

'Jim Braddock! You are some storyteller.'

The older man kept his face free of smiles. 'Reckon if you caught, skinned and treated the pelt of a mountain lion then made it up into a coat for that Rosie gal she'd see her way clear to taking care of you for a week.'

'A week? All that effort must be deserving of more than a week.'

'Careful what you wish for, young Ridgeway. If you insist on more she might regard the gift as a marriage proposal. Then where would you be? What would your father say? He'd probably banish you to this line cabin for a year.'

With his chin tucked inside the upturned collar of his coat Dean chuckled. Men like Jim Braddock never talked about themselves but they always had good stories to tell. The word *marriage* lingered in his mind. Of course he wasn't going to marry Rosie or anyone else from Miss Lily's place, but where else was he going to meet a girl? There were none to be found while riding the range pursuing cows that were only interested in being guided to the next meadow or watering place. The few girls he'd seen in Big Timber hadn't aroused any especial interest and he was seldom permitted to go further afield.

'Have you ever been married, Jim?'

The question took Jim Braddock by surprise and without warning the face of Victoria Saddler appeared in his mind's eye. Demobbed at the end of the war, he'd met and courted her in Pine Bluff, Arkansas. She had been a schoolteacher and, despite his desperate longing to please her, it had soon become apparent that any thoughts of a union between them were doomed to disappointment. She was intelligent in a way he could never emulate and he hadn't the means to provide for her as any good husband should do. He'd accepted every offer of employment that came his way but at that time, in that place, nothing was permanent, there was nothing long term upon which he could hope to build a future.

She'd married a dentist and Jim had moved across the border and taken his first job working with cattle; rounding up the longhorns that roamed wild across the Texas scrubland. Marriage was all right for people like young Dean who weren't handicapped by the lack of intelligence or money, but never again had he considered it. There had been one or two women in his life since then but they had come and gone without prompting thoughts of a permanent life together. Being alone didn't bother him, what irked was the realization that he was forty-six next birthday and had nothing to show for his life but a saddle, a revolver, a Winchester and about two hundred dollars in the Big Timber bank.

Before he could give the lad an answer Dean spoke again.

'Who's that?'

After a first careful mile to let their mounts become accustomed to the tricky ground conditions, they'd picked up the pace as they'd made tracks towards the creek and Fetterman's Brook which marked the boundary between the Broken Arrow and Red Hammer grazing lands. Ahead there were two riders with a dozen cows ahead of them. They'd stopped, waiting, it seemed, for Jim and Dean to approach.

'Red Hammer riders,' Jim muttered, 'with our stock.'

'That looks like Zeb Walters,' Dean said, his eyes fixed on the tall rider on the right. He cast a glance at Jim Braddock, knowing there was bad blood between the two men. Jim had always insisted that it was all on Zeb's part and that the incident, which had occurred on pay day, had been exaggerated by whiskey. Zeb had spent a night in jail and Jim had been told to leave town and stay away until tempers cooled. The banishment wasn't much of a hardship for him; he was hoping and expecting it would be forgotten about as soon as Zeb sobered up.

In the days immediately following the flare-up, it seemed that everyone around Big Timber had an opinion on the root of the problem. Most people said that a woman was to blame, but citing sex as the root of an argument had been in fashion since there had been nothing but snakes in Adam and Eve's garden. One version blamed Zeb Walters for insulting Bluetail Billie, one of the Garter girls who had been a long-time favourite of Jim Braddock, but others blamed it on Jim for trying to take liberties with Zeb's wife. Others had more fanciful explanations, claiming that the argument had been a long time simmering, that the dispute dated back to a time before either man had settled in this part of Montana, but no one had any evidence to support their notion. The card game and Zeb's losses were too insignificant for those who needed a more salacious element to their gossip. But cowboys needed something to jaw about in bar-rooms and to weave stories around for winter nights in the bunkhouse. Attributing blame and innocence was as natural to them as grumbling at cookhouse food, and exaggeration was a competi-tion practised more readily by those who hadn't witnessed the affair.

For Jim Braddock the incident was best forgotten. Zeb, he supposed, who had been the aggressor, would offer to buy him a beer the next time they met and the matter would be closed, but that hadn't been the way of it. The Red Hammer man had not only lost his money but had received a lump on his head and picked up a five-dollar fine. He grumbled to anyone who would listen.

They hadn't seen each other since that day. Without money, Zeb had had no reason to visit Big Timber and although there had been another payday since then, it had coincided with Jim's line-cabin duty. But before riding out to the high boundary Zeb's grumbles had reached Jim's ears and, in the retelling, had become threats of revenge. Now, in awkward silence, they looked at each other. Zeb had his shoulders hunched and his head tilted, making him appear smaller despite the thick mackinaw coat he wore to ward off the chill. In Jim's opinion it was Zeb's place to speak first but the Red Hammer man's lips remained firmly pressed together. Jim couldn't decide if the other's narrow-eyed look expressed anger or contrition. He waited for Zeb to speak but it was the other's companion who uttered the first words.

'We were chasing them back on to your range,' young Harvey Goode explained, waving his hand at the cattle that were milling around a few yards away. His words and the accompanying smile were meant to allay any suspicion the Broken Arrow riders might have had that their stock was being rustled. 'They didn't want to cross the creek. Guess they like

Red Hammer grass better than yours.'

Dean Ridgeway scoffed. 'Well, that just proves you right, Jim. Cows are stupid.'

Harvey laughed, Jim allowed a small smile to tug at his mouth but there was no change to Zeb's expression.

'What do you think, Jim?' Harvey asked, twisting in the saddle to look at the northern sky.

Jim pointed to the Bitterroots in the west, their peaks shrouded in cloud.

'That's snow up there and it's coming this way. Unless you've got four months' provisions in your cabin I think it's time to get out of the high ground. We're going to start on down to the valley as soon as we've rounded up all the stragglers.'

'Don't know that Mr Grisham would welcome us back yet. He reckoned on another month before winter bites.'

'You do what you think is right, Harvey. If you think the man who pays you controls the weather then follow his orders, but this cold and that snow signify a long, harsh winter. We're not hanging around.'

Harvey Goode shrugged in his coat. He cast a glance at his companion to hear his opinion but Zeb was looking at the ground as if he wasn't involved in the conversation. The look Harvey threw at Jim Braddock carried the suggestion that he was to blame for Zeb's voluntary exclusion, that Zeb hadn't yet shucked off the dispute in the Garter. When he spoke again, however, it was to pass on news of another incident in Big Timber, one that had occurred only two days earlier, before the Red Hammer men had been dispatched to their current duty.

'Dan Brix is dead.'

'The deputy?'

'Sure, the deputy. Don't know any other.'

'What happened?' Dean Ridgeway wanted to know.

'Two of his gang broke Frank Felton out of jail. Dan was killed trying to stop them.'

'Did they get away?'

'Yup. Sheriff Stone figures they've gone north into Canada.'

'He got some cause to believe that?'

'That's the way they were heading when they lit out of town. A posse was still hunting them when we came up here.'

Jim looked again at the heavy northern skies.

'If they haven't caught them yet then I don't suppose they will. The townsmen won't risk being cut off in the high country. Snow'll send them skittering home.'

Harvey Goode grunted with amusement at the plight of the posse but didn't comment. Instead he looked back to the hump of land that led down to the boundary creek and said they needed to get back to their own chores. He cast another look at Zeb who still sat morosely silent three or four yards apart from the rest of the group.

'Thanks for sorting out the cattle,' Jim said.

'You'd have done the same for us. See you in Big Timber.' Harvey raised his hand, turned his horse and began to ride away. Zeb began to follow.

'Zeb,' Jim called, and the Red Hammer rider pulled his horse to a halt and looked over his shoulder. 'Is there something on your mind, something you want to say to me?'

The Red Hammer man glowered but remained silent.

'I heard tell you were making threats against me.'

'I got a sore head and a five-dollar fine. What did you get?'

'You were the one making all the noise, Zeb. We've known each other too long to let a poker game and a bottle of whiskey make enemies of us.'

'And twenty dollars.'

'If you didn't want to lose the money you shouldn't have gambled with it.'

Zeb snorted, a derisory sound that suggested that the rift hadn't been healed.

'Next time I see you in Big Timber we'll have a beer together,' Jim offered, but Zeb had wheeled his mount and was riding away to catch up with Harvey.

As he watched them ride up and over the ridge, Jim berated himself for a fool. It had been Zeb's responsibility to make the first move to healing the breach between them. He should have let him go off in his sulky manner; what did it matter if they never spoke again. But it was twenty-two dollars, he told himself; why risk a vendetta for twenty-two dollars?

The Red Hammer men were out of sight now and Jim turned his attention to the few steers that had been returned from across the creek.

'Let's get them moving,' he told Dean, and at that moment a rifle shot cracked behind them.

TWO

From the edge of the ridge Harvey Goode had watched the brief interchange between Jim Braddock and Zeb and waited for his friend to catch up. Zeb rode past, ignoring the younger man, and began the descent down to the creek below. He was at the bottom of the slope before Harvey began to follow. An icy wind gusted down from the high ground and frost still showed white on the frozen ground. Here, the descent to the slim watercourse was about twenty-five feet and Harvey Goode had covered less than a quarter of that distance when an iron-shod hoof skidded on a ice-covered rock. His mount lurched and tried to regain its balance by turning sideways. Harvey leant back to counter the original skid but was jolted forward by the second unexpected movement. The horse went down on its side so quickly that the rider had no opportunity to get out of the saddle. With Harvey's leg trapped against the hard ground the horse slid down the incline. A hideous wail was forced out of Harvey Goode.

Across the creek, Harv's yell brought Zeb to a sudden halt. He twisted in the saddle and looked on helplessly as his comrade's frightened horse slithered down the slope. Despite its frantic efforts the animal was unable to stop its downward momentum. With Harvey crushed against the ground it plunged on to the bank of the creek. Shakily, it got to its feet, shook its head, snorted, then dashed across the creek and past Zeb.

With his wits about him Zeb could have grabbed the reins and calmed the animal, but his eyes were fixed on his companion, who lay silent, twisted and unconscious on the ground. He spurred his horse back across the water and dismounted. Blood smeared the ground marking the line of the horse's descent. Zeb's first impression was that Harv was dead; his eyes were closed and it didn't seem as though he was breathing. His right leg was at a crazy angle. Then there was a moan, barely audible but strong enough to confirm he was alive. Zeb had no idea what he could to do to help the young cowboy.

Then he remembered Jim Braddock. Everyone said that he was resourceful. Perhaps he could help. Grabbing his rifle from its scabbard, he fired a shot in the air. He prayed that the Broken Arrow men would hear and respond. He held the rifle in his hand as he bent to examine the injured man.

*

25

When the first anxiety – that the shot had been fired at them – had been swiftly dismissed, Jim and Dean exchanged enquiring glances.

'Better take a look,' Jim said and, forsaking the small herd, hastened off towards the ridge, Dean tagging along behind.

They stopped on the lip of the treeless escarpment, wary of exposing themselves to a gunman but relieved that no more shots had followed the first. The breath of their horses rose then dissipated in the cold air. The panorama was a predominantly white landscape. Frost covered the ground and clung to the distant trees that marked the location of Fetterman's Brook. The figures of the Red Hammer riders were on the bank of the creek, almost into the little stream of icy water.

Harvey Goode was lying awkwardly on his back, his arms outstretched. Zeb Walters, crouching over him with one knee on the ground, looked up at the riders above. He got to his feet. He was holding the reins of his horse in one hand and his rifle in the other. He raised the arm holding the weapon and beckoned frantically to the Broken Arrow riders. He watched their careful descent to the place where Harvey lay.

'His horse fell.' Zeb threw out the words to Jim and Dean before they had a chance to dismount. 'Lost its footing on the ice and was down before he could get clear.' Jim looked across the creek and could see the animal running with its head high in the way such animals do when governed by nervous

26

panic. 'Harv was trapped underneath as it slid down the hillside. His leg. . . .' Zeb added, sweeping an arm in the direction of his partner, inviting Jim and Dean to inspect it for themselves but clearly unwilling to look upon the damage himself.

Harvey lay so still that Dean Ridgeway was sure he was dead. Jim lifted aside the stricken man's coat to inspect the damage.

'Damnation,' he muttered. The damage to the cowboy's left thigh was grave. It wasn't just broken, it was shattered: a bloody, misshapen mess. Jim looked at Dean, saw the colour drain from the younger fellow's face. 'Succumbed to the pain,' he said.

'What can we do?' asked Zeb.

Jim shook his head. He had no idea what to do. It didn't seem right to move Harvey but he would freeze to death if they didn't get him off the ground. Snow had begun to fall.

'Our shack is closest,' he said, 'we'd better get him there as soon as possible. We've got some laudanum. He'll need it when he comes to his senses.'

No one argued with Jim; wordlessly he was accepted as the leader of the little group. It wasn't a role he ever volunteered to play but it was thrust upon him more and more due to his age and experience. He'd seen broken limbs on several occasions but they had been single, clean breaks. Harvey's leg was shattered. He couldn't begin to estimate how many fractures he'd suffered both above and below the knee. He could see three places where bone had cut through the skin and pierced the material of Harv's trousers.

'What do you want me to do?' Zeb asked again.

In truth, Jim had no idea. He was pretty sure that anything they did would only make matters worse. Harv needed the attention of a proper medical man but that was unlikely to happen for at least another day. It was important, he remembered, to keep the leg straight and still for the healing process to begin but, in this instance, that was impossible. He encircled the leg with a number of stiff twigs and tied them tightly in place to restrict movement, but first he'd had to lift and twist the distorted limb until there was a semblance of normality in its position. As he'd worked the movement of the leg had been unusual: the ball joint, he suspected, had been dislodged from the hip socket. Young Harvey Goode, he figured, wouldn't be asked to chase cows again. Whatever days lay ahead of him they weren't going to be spent at round-ups, cattle drives or riding the line in winter.

Harvey didn't regain consciousness while Jim administered to his leg. Now and then a troubled head movement or deep groan assured everyone that their patient was still alive but all the colour had drained from his face, suggesting that the chance of life's continuity was tenuous. He was laid on a framework of ropes that had been fashioned by Zeb: when it was raised it formed a sling between the two Broken Arrow horses. Dean retrieved a heavy-duty winter oilskin from behind his saddle, which he draped over the comatose cowboy.

'Zeb,' Jim commanded, 'you need to get down to Red Hammer. Send a wagon up to our shack to collect Harv and send another man to fetch Doc Farraday from Big Timber. He needs to be at the ranch when Harv returns.'

Zeb gathered the reins of his mount and climbed into the saddle but Jim put a hand on the bridle before the other could spur his way across the creek. 'Getting help for Harv is urgent,' he said, 'but take it easy, Zeb. Conditions are bad. It won't do anyone any good if you damage yourself or your horse.'

Zeb nodded. 'Thanks for your help, Jim,' he said, the words putting an end to the feud-like relationship that had been developing between them. In an instant, he was gone, his mount splashing through the icy water of the creek and leaving clear tracks in the fresh-fallen snow.

It was almost five miles to the line cabin. Snow was falling steadily and the weather was worsening. Dean drove ahead of him the few head of cattle that the Red Hammer riders had brought across the creek. Jim walked at the heads of the horses carrying Harvey Goode so that he was able to keep them in step and keep an eye on the invalid. It was a weary trudge as the lying snow deepened and the cold began to bite at their faces. Harvey's face was turning blue.

'Will he live?' Dean Ridgeway asked when at last they got him on to the bunk. Transferring him from the sling hadn't been an easy operation and Harv had yelled out his agony even though his eyes hadn't opened and there had been no other symptoms of consciousness.

Jim shrugged, he had no idea. If he had to put money on the outcome it wouldn't have been on the side of survival.

'Keep him warm,' he said, 'that's all that can be done for him, and dose him with laudanum if he wakes.'

'Do we just wait here until someone comes from Red Hammer?'

'*You* do.'

'Me? What are you going to do?'

'Got to check the top ground for your pa's strays.'

Dean flashed a look at the stricken man on the bunk, clearly uncomfortable at the prospect of acting as nursemaid.

'I'll round up the strays,' he offered.

Jim barely acknowledged the other's suggestion with a glance. They both knew that on his own, in the bleak winter whiteness, it was probable that Dean would become more lost than the cattle.

Dean ventured the thought that there might not be any strays up by the Indian burial ground. 'Even if there are, what's the loss of a couple of cows?'

'Those couple of cows are the reason we've been sent up here,' Jim reminded him. 'Your pa would rather lose me than a couple of cows.' Jim thought that probably wasn't true but the old man would never admit it.

'I don't know what to do here,' Dean complained.

'No more do I,' Jim confessed. 'Like I told you, keep him warm. If he develops a fever, wipe his brow. If he wakes in agony give him a dose of laudanum. We've got nothing else.'

The ranch owner's son wasn't happy with the situation but he didn't have the necessary ammunition with which to fight Jim Braddock. He regarded the awkwardly still figure on the bunk as an unarguable reason for having nothing to do with a life chasing cows.

'How long will you be gone?' he asked.

'Can't tell,' Jim replied. 'I'll be back as soon as possible. If they get the wagon here before I return just wait for me. We'll try to get back to the ranch tomorrow. We haven't enough provisions to stay here much longer.'

THREE

Although there were black, snow-filled clouds overhead, none had travelled further south to shed their load in the valley below. As he worked his way hesitantly across the hillside Zeb Walters could see that the valley floor still retained the dull green colour of late-autumn grass. It was a sight that gave him encouragement, hope that soon there would be no need for him to maintain the tentative pace he had so far adopted; he would be able to put his mount to the gallop that the situation required. When he pictured in his mind the damage done to Harvey Goode's leg he doubted if it would ever be of any use to the young man again; then, recalling the ghastly expression on Harv's face, he knew that survival itself would be a miracle. Jim Braddock had insisted that he would only be saved by treatment from a qualified doctor, and even that might not be enough, but Zeb was determined to do his utmost to save the lad's life.

As he rode his thoughts dwelt on Jim Braddock.

For weeks he'd been ashamed of the way he'd involved the Broken Arrow man in his personal tribulations. None of the other Red Hammer riders had spoken outright about the incident in The Garter, but there had been comments implying that he would now be dead if Sheriff Stone hadn't clubbed him when he did. Despite that, he'd still tried to insinuate that Jim had cheated. No one believed him. Jim Braddock might never amount to anything more than a drover on a cattle ranch but he'd never shown any desire to be anything else. Around Big Timber he was respected for his past experience and current contentment.

That, in Zeb's opinion, was where he and Jim Braddock differed. Perhaps they were of equal status on their respective spreads, senior hands capable of undertaking tasks with very little supervision, but Zeb had come to Montana having already failed to establish himself as a homesteader in Nebraska and that failure had gnawed at his sense of self-worth. When his yield had been poor he found cause to blame the land, the climate and his tools, but deep down he knew that the fault lay with none of those. It was an accepted fact that Nebraskan farmland was so fertile that a good farmer could plough a straight line from sunup to sundown; they'd had four of the mildest winters in living memory; and he couldn't blame the equipment because he'd invested in the latest tools. The fault was his; he had the ambition but not the ability to be a farmer.

He'd brought his wife and daughter west, claiming that he would succeed in Montana where he'd failed in Nebraska. The house he'd bought on the outskirts of Big Timber was supposed to be a temporary home until they found a suitable strip of land to farm, but he'd gone to work for Charlie Grisham's Red Hammer outfit and after eight years was still there, reaping forty dollars a month for his labour and loyalty. In the meantime, his wife, Alice, had earned money by spells of taking in laundry, dressmaking and baking cakes and pies that were sold by the owner of Big Timber's emporium. Jane, Zeb's eighteen-year-old daughter, now worked in the emporium and they projected the image of a settled family.

From time to time, however, both Zeb and Alice recognized that the early ambitions of their marriage had not been achieved and both blamed the failure on Zeb. That had been his mood when he'd sat at the card table opposite Jim Braddock that payday, with something in his psyche telling him that a big poker win would mollify Alice and prove to himself that he could support his family. It hadn't worked out that way. He'd lost more than twenty dollars, incurred a five-dollar fine and spent a night in jail with a lump on his head. In addition, he'd tried to shift the blame for it all on to Jim Braddock. To cover his own weakness he'd almost accused Jim of cheating and had made comments for which some men might seek retribution.

Yet Jim Braddock had barely referred to the

matter, had, indeed, offered an olive branch, and Zeb knew that the Broken Arrow man wasn't afraid of him. He was simply confident and capable, so capable that he could even admit that he didn't know what to do to help Harv, then set about issuing instructions to get the injured lad to a place of warmth and send a rider for help. He, Zeb, hadn't known what to do either, but he'd merely stood around looking at the unconscious man and his mangled leg.

That was the difference; Jim knew his limitations and worked around them while he, Zeb, knew his limitations and succumbed to them. He pricked the flank's of his pony, urged it on; he wouldn't let anyone down this day.

Zeb had almost covered the eight miles back to the line cabin that he and Harv had shared when he caught sight of a riderless horse off to his left. It was Harv's mount, returning instinctively to the place of shelter it had known for the last few nights. It crossed Zeb's mind to catch it: a second horse might be an asset on the long run to the ranch house when he reached the floor of the valley, but, having reached this lower plateau, his own mount was now settled into a ground-eating rhythm that he was reluctant to interrupt. Half a dozen strides later, however, he did just that. Something else had caught his eye.

The cabin had been built close to the hillside and within a sharp recess, to provide protection from the ravages of winter. A stand of trees acted as a westerly windbreak and obscured its existence from anyone travelling from that direction. Now, above those trees, a thin column of smoke could be seen; it could only be coming from the stove within the hut.

Puzzled, Zeb halted his mount. He and Harv had decided not to bank up the stove before leaving that morning. They had planned a long day along the creek, sorting out cattle and chasing Broken Arrow strays back on to their own range and no matter how much wood they put in, the fire would certainly have burned out before their return. By now the fire should be no more than embers at best. Someone else had to be using the cabin for so much smoke to be rising into the air. The obvious candidate was a rider with a message from the ranch owner. The unexpected possibility of having an ally near at hand cheered Zeb. Perhaps the newcomer could provide some practical assistance in the care of Harvey Goode, or could take the news down to the ranch so that he, Zeb, could return to the line cabin on the Broken Arrow range. Snow began to fall again as Zeb turned his horse in the direction of the cabin.

Harv's mount had paused at the end of the tree line, its black form a stark image in the falling snow. Its head was high and its breath made misty grey trails in the air. Zeb kicked on towards it. After grabbing its bridle he turned his attention to the cabin about fifty yards distant. Instead of the solitary mount of a messenger from the ranch, he was surprised to see four horses tied to the hitching post.

He paused a moment, studied the horses and knew that none of them belonged to the Red Hammer string. Curious, but boosted by his belief that the visitors were allies, he quickly satisfied himself of their identity. They had to be members of the Big Timber posse sent out to recapture Frank Felton. It was possible that among them was someone with greater medical knowledge than he or Jim Braddock possessed. Leading Harv's horse, he made his way towards the shack. He was only halfway across the clearing when the door opened.

A man, huddled in a long leather coat with his wide-brimmed hat low on his brow, stepped outside. As he emerged he threw words over his shoulder, back into the cabin, then looked up at the dark sky with annoyance. For several moments he was unaware of the approaching rider, the lying snow already muffling the sound of the horses' hoofs on the hard ground. Pushing between two of the tethered horses he prepared to unsaddle one of them but at that moment looked up and over the animal's back and ceased his task before it had truly begun.

He shouted back to the cabin: 'Phipps,' but a second man had already emerged and his gaze was fixed steadily on the oncoming horseman.

At the appearance of the second man Zeb Walters pulled on the reins and stopped his mount's progress. He hadn't recognized the first man to leave the shack but that wasn't surprising: he was wrapped up against the cold so that his features weren't easily discernible. Besides, Big Timber was a growing community, Zeb no longer knew every man who lived there. This, he guessed, was some stolid citizen who had felt it his duty to join the posse. But his sight of the man who now stood in the doorway of the line cabin revised Zeb's assumption.

Gus Phipps wasn't a man he'd ever spoken to but the features of his long face had been printed in newspapers and displayed on wanted posters throughout the territory. The black patch covering his left eye left no doubt in Zeb's mind that the man he was looking at was Frank Felton's right-hand man. The men in the cabin weren't members of the posse, they were the men the posse was hunting.

A long-barrelled Colt suddenly filled the hand of the one-eyed outlaw. Zeb jerked the head of his mount and turned it away from the line cabin. A shot sounded: the deeper report of a rifle, and Zeb felt the bullet tug at the shoulder of his heavy winter coat. He stretched forward, getting his body closer to his horse to make himself a smaller target. Two more shots sounded and he threw a look backwards as he urged the horses in flight away from the guns.

Smoke was rising from the pistol in Gus Phipps's hand and from the end of the rifle that the other man now had resting across the saddle of the horse he was stationed behind. A third man had emerged from the cabin and soon all three were scrambling to mount their horses. They meant to pursue Zeb, hunt him down and kill him. Zeb yelled in his horse's ear and pricked its flanks with his rough spurs as they raced for the edge of the plateau to the timber and prairie land below.

Zeb kept his horse running flat out; the caution that had governed the first portion of his ride was now cast aside; slipping in the snow was a secondary consideration to the risk of a bullet in the back. He had a head start on his pursuers and was, he suspected, more familiar with the territory, but that was an advantage nullified by the snow. His tracks were easy to follow; he had to get below the snowline before the outlaws caught him.

Occasionally, he cast a glance behind him. Twice he saw the threesome in relentless pursuit and knew that the gap between him and them was diminishing. There had been no more shots fired but he figured they wouldn't want to advertise their presence in case the posse was within hearing distance. Gunshots, he thought, were to his advantage.

When he next saw his pursuers they were less than a quarter of a mile behind. He fired two shots in the air and saw the trio pull their horses to a halt. Perhaps he'd fooled them into thinking he was signalling for assistance, or perhaps they'd decided it was too risky to continue the chase any closer to the ranches and settlements. The tree line was within sight. Zeb heaved a sigh of relief. He'd outrun them.

There was no snow on the ground among the trees, nor had it fallen on the rangeland he needed to cross. If he was smart it would be easy to lose the men on his trail as he headed for the Red Hammer ranch. But he was confident that they would no longer continue the pursuit. He'd dismounted to give his horse a breather but he knew he couldn't delay too long. Getting word to the sheriff that Frank Felton and his men were in the territory around Fetterman's Pool was important but, for him and the people at Red Hammer, getting help for Havey Goode was more so. It was only when he relaxed for a moment that he realized he'd been wounded by the bullet that had tugged at his coat. It wasn't a serious wound but it was stinging and, he suspected, bleeding. He'd been holding the reins of Harvey Goode's horse but now he released them, allowed the animal to run free, knowing it would follow when he set out on the last leg of the trip to the ranch house.

When he broke from the tree line on to the open pasture his thoughts were fixed on the weather and the possibility of getting a wagon back up to the Broken Arrow line cabin before nightfall. He would go back with them, he decided, Harv was his partner and he should be with him.

The bullet smashed into his back. He threw his hands in the air before pitching forward along his horse's neck, then tumbling slowly to the ground at its feet. The horse stopped and waited for its rider to remount; when he didn't, it began to munch the tough grass.

Among the trees Gus Phipps watched for a moment, then, when his victim didn't move, he slid his rifle back into its scabbard, turned his animal and followed the hoofprints in the snow back to the rest of the gang. He didn't know if the man he'd just killed was a cowboy or a member of the posse that was chasing them, but it no longer mattered, he wasn't going to pass on what he knew to anyone else. Still, Phipps thought, they could no longer stay in that cabin. They needed to get out quickly, cross the border into Canada where they would be safe for a while.

FOUR

His horse's reluctance to tackle the higher ground when Jim Braddock turned its head to the north was obvious and understandable. Dark clouds covered the highest mountain peaks indicative of heavy falling snow. Like its rider, the beast beneath him sensed that it would soon be calamitous to be exposed on the open hillside. Jim calculated that they had less than two hours to get back to the shelter of the cabin where he'd left Dean Ridgeway nursing Harvey Goode. He wasn't sure that that gave him enough time to climb as high as the burial ground but not for a moment did he entertain any thought of not pressing ahead. He took money to tend Hec Ridgeway's stock so that was what he would do. Cows hadn't the sense to move away from an oncoming storm, they just sat down and waited for it to pass. That was why, if someone like him didn't chivvy them along, they froze to death and were eaten by wolves. Jim pulled the collar of his coat closer to the back of his neck and coaxed the beast beneath him onwards.

He had ridden back towards the creek that separated the Broken Arrow land from its neighbour but reached it a few miles north of the spot where the meeting with Zeb and Harvey had taken place. So far he hadn't found any cattle or any sign of them. Perhaps there weren't any other strays to find, but it wasn't his place to make assumptions. He pushed north towards the old Sioux burial ground, where there were one or two small valleys and ravines into which other cattle had wandered over the years. That was the last place to search, then he would return to the cabin as quickly as possible.

A strong gust of icy wind carried snow into his face. While he rode he wrapped a scarf around his head in such fashion as to keep his hat secured to his head and keep his ears warm. As he tied it under his chin he wondered about the chances of help reaching them before the snow became too deep. It was difficult enough for a wagon to reach the outlying cabins without that additional handicap. But Jim was a practical man and knew there was nothing he could do to amend the situation.

At that moment a movement at the other side of the creek caught his attention. He halted and focused on the distant dark shapes. He counted seven riders, too many to be Red Hammer hands this far from the ranch. Posse-men, he figured, still hunting for the escaped outlaw, but then he saw a pennant fluttering and realized that there was a semblance of order in the group's formation. He hadn't seen a cavalry patrol in this area for seven years, not since 1877 when the 'Christian General' Howard's army had harried Chief Joseph's Nez Percé into starvation among these hills.

Although he knew they were only obeying orders, Jim Braddock had had little empathy with the conduct of those soldiers, but he hoped that the ones that he could now see across the narrow water channel would be able to provide assistance. Among them, he hoped, might be someone with more medical ability than he and Dean possessed.

The leader of the patrol was a young lieutenant called Cooper who, for gravitas, wore a long moustache. With an upraised hand he halted the men in his wake when he saw the approaching rider. Despite the long overcoats that each man wore it was clear that they weren't happy in the cold conditions.

After introducing himself Jim told the cavalry officer of his need.

'A man's injured,' he said, 'his leg's crushed and he needs more attention than my partner and I can give him. Can you come and take a look at him? Perhaps one of your men has some experience with battlefield injuries?'

A sergeant had ridden forward to sit alongside the officer while he spoke to the civilian. He was an older man, with experience, no doubt, of the foibles of young officers. However, he didn't speak, merely waited for the lieutenant to seek his advice.

Jim allowed his eyes to sweep over the remainder

of the patrol. It was difficult to see their faces; most of them were hidden behind turned up collars and the yellow bandannas that had been employed to protect their cheeks and jaws from the biting cold, but, apart from the sergeant, there was just such an expression in their unhappy eyes as to make their military inexperience a certainty. They were young, weary and cold and eager to be a long way from the Montana hillside on which they had halted.

Even while Jim's glance was taking in the men of the patrol Lieutenant Cooper's words were confirming his thoughts.

'Can't help you, Mr Braddock. Even if I had anyone capable of treating your friend I couldn't spare him. Some Sioux have quit the reservation and we have to get them back before they stir up any trouble.'

'Sioux?' Jim's voice was heavy with incredulity. 'There aren't any around here.' Jim knew that that wasn't the absolute truth; one or two former tribesmen worked as horse wranglers on the bigger spreads and some Americans living on isolated farms had taken a Sioux woman as a wife, but there were no hostile warriors of the type these soldiers were seeking.

'A bunch led by Grey Eagle escaped the Pine Ridge Agency. They were heading in this direction.'

The name held no significance for Jim. He looked up at the dark, threatening sky and wondered what lunacy would cause a handful of warriors to endure the coming winter weather with very little to protect or shelter them.

As if reading Jim's thoughts Lieutenant Cooper spoke again.

'Grey Eagle is confined to the reservation. Leaving is a breach of his parole for which he and those assisting him will be punished.'

Jim looked at the sergeant as though expecting the older man to confirm his own reading of the situation.

'Even when they were roving free the Sioux didn't make war at this time of year,' he told the lieutenant.

'They've raided farms on their way west,' the officer told him. 'That's how we've been able to trail them.'

'Anyone hurt?'

'No, and we mean to catch them before someone is. They will be treated as hostiles and I'll demand their unconditional surrender.'

Jim Braddock looked again at the men of the patrol. It struck him that seven inexperienced soldiers made a feeble force to put in the field against a Sioux war party.

'My advice, Lieutenant,' he said, 'is to get back down to the valley.'

The cavalry officer bristled, sensing criticism of his command.

'Is that the advice of an old Indian fighter?' he asked.

'No, it's the advice of a man who has lived in this territory for many years.' Jim pointed to the black sky ahead. 'Snow,' he announced, 'and if this is the early onset of winter then it'll come tumbling out of the sky for weeks on end. Even if you are on the right trail you're unlikely to find any Sioux up here, but if you get cut off you'll probably meet your Maker.'

'The army doesn't surrender at the first sign of adversity, mister,' the peeved lieutenant told him.

'I'm trying to help you,' Jim told him. 'The army can't do much with seven frozen corpses. Go to my cabin. Drink some coffee, then take a look at my friend. Perhaps you can figure a way to get him down to the ranch without too much discomfort.'

Jim needed nothing more than the fixed expression on the lieutenant's face to inform him that his advice would be ignored, but the soldier put it into words.

'We have our duty to do,' he said; then, sounding more conciliatory, 'I wish you luck finding assistance for your friend.'

'Sir,' the sergeant interrupted, 'we have a little laudanum among our supplies. We can probably spare a little to ease the man's suffering.'

'Thank you, Sergeant,' Jim said, 'but that's the one thing we have ourselves. For now, it's keeping Harv unconscious.'

The lieutenant raised his hand, prepared to advance with his small force, anxious to get the impatient horses moving again.

'I reckon the snow will hit us in little more than an hour,' Jim said. 'There are caves up there. Try to

47

find one and wait for it to stop. You'll get lost if you try to keep going in a blizzard.'

The lieutenant waved his upraised arm, the sergeant gave a nod of his head to acknowledge Jim's advice, then the seven men rode off slowly into the gathering gloom.

Jim recrossed the creek and followed his own northerly trail. The steadily falling snow was making the uphill journey more difficult but there was a small shelf of land that gave a view across the stretch of territory where the upland cattle tended to assemble. If he could gain that height it might obviate the need to go any further. If there were no cattle to be seen there wouldn't be any need to proceed into those ravines. The horse shivered, shaking snow and water from its coat, then it took slow, careful steps, its legs disappearing hock-deep into the unspoilt snow carpet. It took twenty minutes and the snow was now sweeping down in gusts that made conditions almost blizzard like, but eventually he gained the position he sought and looked over a white hillside upon which nothing moved.

Here and there the lee side of a leafless tree showed stark black against the whiteness of the landscape and the mound of a snow-covered rock broke the monotony of an otherwise featureless terrain. Jim sat for a moment, not regretting the absence of cattle and therefore a speedy return to the cabin. Thoughts raced across his mind concerning Dean and Harvey and how far Zeb Walters might have got on his run to the Red Hammer ranch. He deemed it unlikely that they would try to get a wagon up to the cabin before morning. He and Dean would have to do their best to keep Harv pain-free until his bunkmates got him to a doctor.

His other concern was the cavalry patrol. He hoped the lieutenant had taken his advice and found somewhere to shelter. The sergeant, he told himself, was an old hand at army patrols and would no doubt persuade the officer to do the right thing. These were no conditions for anyone to be adrift in the hills. At least, he thought, there were no cattle. He'd done all that was required of a top hand; now it was time to look after himself.

As he began to turn his horse something moved off to his right. He caught a glimpse of brown in the corner of his eye but when he turned his head there was nothing to see. He scanned the unspoilt, white terrain. He grunted, allowed himself a grumble about dumb lost cows, then tapped his heels against the horse and let it pick a path down from the shelf to the lower valley.

Jim had pinpointed a mound behind which he expected to find the stray if what he had seen was such an animal. The closer he got the less confident he was that he wasn't just on a wild-goose chase. Perhaps it had been some bird, an eagle perhaps, whose flight had flicked across his line of vision creating an image distorted by the heavy snowfall. But there had been no repetition of the movement. Would a cow stay still so long?

It took almost five minutes to work his way to the mound. The only sound was the creak of his saddle leather and the occasional dull chink of the metal bits of the head harness. He scoured the ground; there were no tracks in the snow and he grumbled more loudly for allowing himself to be duped by a mirage and wasting precious time in getting off the mountain. Still, he'd come this far and it wasn't in his nature to leave a job a half done. He'd reached the mound and began to walk his horse around it, checking that the critter hadn't slipped and injured itself in the snow.

Small indentations in the snow were the first signs to catch his attention; not marks of a four-legged animal but more like small human footprints, which had been almost obliterated by the fresh snow. He worked his animal slowly around the snow-covered boulder and stopped in amazement when he reached the far side. It seemed as though an eye, big and black, had opened in the snow like some supernatural spectre. It watched him and he, shaking off the first unsettling sensation, studied it.

Eventually he identified the head of a white horse, then its neck; he realized that it was lying down and snow had piled up over its body. Behind it a tent had been formed by covering a shaky frame with a blanket, which was now sagging under the weight of snow it was collecting. Within that structure a small face with large, frightened eyes looked out at him. A dull red blanket covered the girl's head but her dark features denoted her as Sioux.

50

'Good God,' said Jim. 'What on earth are you doing there?' His mind had already associated her with the group that the cavalry patrol were seeking.

The only answer he received was the threat of a rifle barrel pushed through the snow.

'You don't need that,' he said. 'I'm not going to hurt you.'

Unblinking, the eyes remained fixed on him.

'Do you understand me?' Although she didn't speak Jim was certain that the girl understood English. He dipped his head forward as another heavy squall of snow blew into his face.

'You can't stay there,' he said, 'and you need to get your pony on to its feet. It might be providing a bit of warmth at the moment but if it lies there too long it won't be able to get up again and it'll freeze to death. Then you'll be stuck up here without any means of getting off the mountain. You don't want to die up here alone.'

Still the girl didn't speak. A little of the fear that had predominated in the look in her dark eyes had been replaced by a hint of indecision, as though she was battling with herself between a tribal distrust of the horseman and acceptance of the truth in his words. She gestured with the rifle, ordering him to go away.

Once again Jim tried to reason with the girl.

'I don't mean you any harm,' he told her. 'You'll die if you stay here. There's a cabin a short distance away where you'll be warm.' He pointed down the hillside to indicate its position. The resulting emphatic headshake confirmed her understanding of English but didn't offer Jim Braddock much hope of winkling her out of her encampment. He made one final effort.

'There's a cave close by,' he told her, trying to keep his voice friendly but needing to shout to make his words audible against the rising wind. 'You can stay there until this storm is over.' It was clear that the girl was tempted by that suggestion. 'It's big enough for you and the pony. I'll light a fire for you, but we need to do it now before you become too cold to move.'

The girl looked away, calculating, Jim supposed, between capture and return to the reservation or certain death. After a moment she withdrew the rifle and Jim stepped down to get the pony back on its feet. As he brushed the snow off the snorting, trembling beast he could see the girl on her knees within the small structure she'd built. She had her back to him and although the red blanket that covered her head reached down her back there was only the skirt of her buckskin dress covering the lower part of her body. On her feet were ankle-high moccasins but between those and the fringed hem of her dress, her legs were bare. He was still looking at them, still in awe of her fortitude, when she turned her head to look at him over her shoulder. She knew he was her looking at her bare legs but misinterpreted the expression on his face. Resentment flashed in her eyes and her hand moved towards the rifle. It was clear that she was determined to defend herself to the death.

Jim Braddock raised open hands to show he had only peaceful intentions but the smile he tried to put on his face didn't develop. Until that moment he hadn't realized that the girl was not alone. Behind her, wrapped in a thick brown bearskin, lay an old man. The darkness of his skin was tinged with grey, his lips were blue and his eyes were closed. There was no movement and Jim was sure that the man was dead.

FIVE

Frank Fenton wasn't as impressed with the work of his top gunman as the man himself. In his usual manner, Gus Phipps had bragged about the killing of the lone rider when he'd returned to the line cabin that the outlaws were occupying.

'You're sure he's dead?' Frank had asked.

'I don't miss,' replied the other. 'He won't tell anyone where we are.'

'Perhaps not,' Frank had agreed, 'but Sheriff Ben Stone isn't a fool. He'll link us to the killing and know that we must be holed up somewhere near by. I don't know how many of these line cabins have been built around here but I suspect they'll be the first places he sends men to check out.'

'It might be days before the body is found. Punchers spend weeks alone in these remote places.'

Frank Felton produced arguments against Gus's complacency.

'Sometimes punchers work in pairs. Another one

might turn up at any moment.'

'Then he'll get the same welcome,' Phipps replied with a grin.

'But he might not turn up single-handed. There were gunshots fired. Someone could have heard them. Possibly the sheriff's posse. Choctaw tells me the man fired shots in the air when you were chasing him.'

Phipps flicked his hand in a dismissive gesture. 'The ruse of a doomed man.'

'Or a signal,' snapped the outlaw leader. 'Even-money chance he was with the posse and that by now they've found his body and are following tracks in the snow that lead straight to us.'

Gus Phipps didn't like the implied criticism: that everyone was in danger because of his actions. He pulled out his Colt and spun it on his index finger.

'Storekeepers and clerks. How accurate are they going to be?'

'They don't need to be accurate. You killed that deputy so Stone's probably armed every man with a shotgun and there'll be enough of them to blow a hole in these shaky walls.'

Frank gazed around the room, holding the gaze of each man in turn. He owed them for springing him from the Big Timber jailhouse but that was because he'd led them successfully in the past and they had expected him to do so in the future. Things were different now.

The deputy hadn't been the only one to collect lead that day. As they'd ridden out of town Frank, too, had been hit and the bullet was still somewhere in his gut. It caused him pain when he moved and he'd lost a lot of blood. The proof of the damage, he reckoned, was etched on his face for all to see and they were, no doubt, summing up his worth to them in the future. Choctaw Jennings had bandaged him up as best he was able but that hadn't done much to ease his suffering.

He'd hoped to remain in this shack for a few days, hoping that the rest would revive him enough to cope with the long journey ahead, but now they would have to move; it was too risky to stay here any longer. The problem was how far could he get before he became a liability to the others and would they desert him when the posse closed in?

He looked at the three men, Gus Phipps, Choctaw Jennings and Drum Hayes, and knew that in other circumstances he would sacrifice any of them to save his own skin. But for now he needed them and couldn't allow his leadership to slip away.

'We've got to go,' he told them.

Gus and Drum rummaged through the cabin and loaded the stock of tinned food, coffee beans, flour and bacon that they found into a canvas bag. Meanwhile Choctaw, working under Frank's grey-faced, wide-eyed scrutiny, tended the gang leader's wound. His silence when he exposed the gaping hole in Frank's belly was a more telling statement than any that he could have expressed with words. He mopped away the blood that had flowed on to the surrounding skin and renewed the bandages, but they too were darkening with fresh blood before Frank had refastened his shirt.

'Perhaps we should stay here another day,' Choctaw said.

'Do you think I'll heal in that time, Choctaw?' Frank Felton's tone was both sarcastic and belligerent. 'Or perhaps you think that by the morning I'll be too weak to prevent you leaving me here to die.'

'I was thinking that being jostled on the back of a horse is going to be hell for you. It won't cure you, but you might garner some strength from a night's rest.'

Frank wasn't sure he believed in Choctaw's concern but he knew he was the one man among his followers who didn't harbour a desire to be leader. When the time came to make a decision about his fate it would probably be Gus Phipps who took it. Gus would assume he was the next leader because of his speed on the draw, but he couldn't think beyond the end of his gun barrel. Drum Hayes was the most capable man but Frank figured that if Gus realized that then Drum might as well be walking around with a target pinned to his chest.

The decision had been taken to keep to the easier trails through the foothills and head north for Canada, but Choctaw had argued against it. He was in favour of cutting westward, through the mountain passes to Butte. His main cause for concern was the lack of settlements to the north and the near certainty that none of those that they did come across would boast the presence of a proper doctor capable of removing the bullet in Frank's gut. He also pointed out that, going north, they would be more likely to run into the posse that had been organized to find them. The members of that makeshift group would be reluctant to search among the many ravines and valleys of the mountains. After their initial outrage following the killing of Deputy Brix, they would be anxious to attend to their everyday business. But Choctaw got no support, not even from Frank who would benefit most.

Nature, however, provided a much more compelling argument for not travelling north. They hadn't gone more than quarter of a mile before it became obvious that they weren't likely to make much progress in that direction. Gusts of wind drove the snow into their faces, soaking them, freezing them and making it difficult to keep their eyes open as their reluctant horses trudged ahead. So heavy was the falling snow that visibility was little more than twenty yards.

Drum Hayes cursed and gathered the other three around him.

'We've got to find shelter,' he announced. 'Choctaw's right, we'll be better off in the mountains. There are deserted mine shacks and caves up there where we can see out this storm. It's bound to relent in a day or two and by then the posse will certainly be back in Big Timber. We'll be able to travel more freely.'

'What if it doesn't?' Gus Phipps wanted to know.

'Then we make other plans. Go west to Butte or

Missoula, but this snow is sweeping down from the Canadian grasslands and we'd be crazy to ride into it.'

Choctaw didn't speak, just gave a curt nod of agreement, his earlier argument was now vindicated, the cold rendering needless any inclination to crow about his judgement.

Frank Felton also remained silent. His head was deep into hunched shoulders. Eyes, half-closed, were the only feature of his face that could be seen. His hat was fastened tight to his head by means of its chin string and the big collar of his heavy coat was upturned to protect the back of his neck and his ears. A scarf was wrapped around the lower portion of his face but already it was thick with the snow that had driven against him on the short ride.

His companions waited for a moment in expectation of a decision from their leader, but it soon became clear that Frank no longer had the ability to command. Back at the cabin, mounting his horse had been an ordeal but once in the saddle he had insisted he was capable of undertaking the journey north. Now it was clear he could not continue. His current motionlessness indicated that not only was he unable to offer any guidance to his men but had probably not even heard Drum's suggestion. He was like a corpse frozen in the saddle.

The other three looked at each other, each aware that Frank Felton was unlikely ever to see Canada. Drum Hayes swung his horse and led the way westward. Gus Phipps followed. Choctaw grabbed the bridle of Frank's horse and led it along in their wake.

For a few minutes they paused in the shelter of the trees around Fetterman's Pool. Nothing moved across the surrounding landscape and they were content to believe that the severe winter weather would be enough to drive the posse back to Big Timber. No one would have been prepared for such a ferocious snowfall. They ate some of the biscuits they'd brought from the shack but Drum said they'd have to be careful with the provisions because they couldn't be sure when they'd find more.

They followed the creek for a little way, hoping that it would provide some shelter from the worst of the weather but in fact it served as a channel along which the wind blew and the snow flew. It was when they were climbing out of the small valley that Frank groaned and swayed and would have fallen out of the saddle if Choctaw hadn't reacted swiftly. He called to the other two, who paused and watched Choctaw from the lip of the rise as he ministered to the wounded man.

Frank Felton seemed to have shrunk during the journey. His hunch-shouldered form leaned forward so that his chest was almost touching his saddle horn. His moans were deep and pain-filled and his eyes, although open, seemed glazed and unseeing. But it was the dark specks on the scarf that gave Choctaw most cause for concern. Frank Felton was coughing up blood, and for that there was probably no cure. Choctaw held Frank in the saddle as they climbed up to the rim to join the other two.

'He can't go much further,' he told them. 'We need to find a place where he can rest.'

Gus Phipps grinned unpleasantly; his solution to the problem was clear to discern. Frank Felton was dying, so *just push him off his horse.* Within an hour he would be dead where he lay, covered with snow, undiscovered until spring or dragged off to be a wolf pack's dinner.

The same sort of thought flitted through the mind of Drum Hayes, but they'd taken a risk in rescuing their leader from his jail cell and somehow it seemed as though abandoning him now would amount to failure. Still, when he twisted in his saddle to survey the surrounding terrain it was clear to him that they were unlikely to find shelter in the immediate vicinity.

'Let's go,' was all he said.

It was almost an hour later when they reached the Broken Arrow line cabin. Dean Ridgeway had coffee simmering in a pot on the round-bellied stove and was considering pouring out another mugful for himself. The availability of the hot drink was, in his opinion, the only advantage pertaining to the task of being a nursemaid. He would have preferred to be out chasing cows in thick snow to being stuck in this warm cabin with an injured man. He knew nothing of doctoring and was terrified of the responsibility that had been put on him. He could live with himself if he made a mess of a task involving cows, he wasn't sure he could if his bungling cost another man his life.

Twice the Red Hammer rider had approached full consciousness, the first moans of discomfort rising to piercing screams of agony when he tried to move his shattered leg. Nervously, Dean had prepared a dose of laudanum in the manner prescribed by Jim Braddock. This had dulled the pain and rendered the sufferer unconscious. From time to time Dean had looked out of the shack's single window, hoping to see his partner returning from his tour of the high plateau, but all he'd seen was snow and he began to wonder if Jim Braddock would ever return.

Dean jumped up, startled by the violent opening of the door as it swung right back and slammed against the wall. He was on the verge of exercising his authority as the ranch owner's son by berating Jim Braddock for the noisy entrance and for leaving him for so long with a task he disliked, when he realized that the man standing in the doorway wasn't the one considered to be one of his father's top riders.

On another occasion, at another time and in another place, the newcomer might have presented a comic figure: snow was piled high on his hat and was crusted on to his long coat, making him look like a sugar-coated gingerbread man. All else, however, betokened a man of violence. His stance, his left leg ahead of his right in the manner of prizefighters whom Dean had seen at Fourth of July celebrations in Miles City, suggested he was ready either to repel or launch an attack. His head remained steady, his face was red and wet from the snow but his narrowed eyes searched the room, taking in every detail. He held a rifle in his hands, the hammer back and a gloved finger tight inside the trigger-guard. He stared at Dean without emotion, unnerving the younger man who had already been startled by the turbulent entrance.

'Who are you?' Dean asked.

His question was ignored as three more men came through the doorway, one supported between the other two. Their expressions were no less grim than that of the man with the rifle as they scanned the small room for somewhere to rest their wounded companion.

With a jerk of his rifle Drum Hayes indicated the place where Harvey Goode lay.

'We need that cot.'

'He can't be moved. His leg's bust,' Dean protested.

'Get him out,' Drum insisted.

Dean Ridgeway looked at each of the men in turn. He knew they weren't going to listen to reason but he had nothing else to offer.

'He was crushed under his horse,' he explained. 'His thigh is shattered. He can't stand.'

Gus Phipps, who was holding on to Frank Felton with his left hand, shuffled aside the skirt of his long coat to enable Dean to see the long Colt that was strapped to his leg.

'We don't care,' he told the rancher's son, 'just get him out so that our friend can lie down.'

Only then did notions as to the identities of the intruders begin to form in Dean's mind. He couldn't recall the name of the man with the eyepatch, whose face had been represented quite frequently in recent newspapers, but he did know that he was one of the associates of Frank Felton. They had killed Deputy Dan Brix to get the outlaw out of jail and Dean had no doubt that they would kill again to preserve their freedom.

So when he spoke again in words that seemed to reflect a determination to oppose them, they were merely a reflection of his nervousness and an inability to assemble his thoughts into more practicable action.

'He's drugged,' he said. 'Unconscious with laudanum.'

Drum Hayes swung his rifle by the barrel and smashed the butt into Dean's stomach. The young man grunted as the wind was forced out of his body, then sank to his knees. A second swing of the rifle brought the butt to collide with the back of Dean's head, felling him to stretch out stunned on the floor. For the next few minutes everything was hazy but, through the pain and nausea, Dean was still able to hang on to enough sense to know what was happening. He knew that it was Harvey Goode's piteous wails that enabled him to do so, a recognition that the agony visited upon the Red Hammer cowboy was so great that it had pierced the deadening effect of the laudanum. Dean's instinct was to go to his aid but no matter how he struggled to shake

64

off the effect of the blows he'd taken, he was unable to gain enough strength to get up off the floor.

Drum Hayes voice sounded above Harv's wretched wails, grumbling to nobody in particular.

'Someone stop that noise.'

'Only one way to do that.' It was Gus Phipps who spoke and although he kept his voice low he couldn't disguise the hint of pleasure it contained. 'Want me to take care of it?'

Drum cast a look at the tormented figure that had been dragged off the cot and dumped on the floor.

'You wouldn't keep a horse alive if it had injuries like those. He won't be of use to anybody ever again.'

'Kindest thing to do,' said Gus drawing his gun.

'Not in here,' Drum told him, 'and don't make a noise.'

'There's nobody else around,' Gus argued. 'There's not room for more than two line riders in a cabin like this and there won't be anyone coming to visit them in this weather.'

'I was thinking of the posse,' Drum argued.

'Forget them. They've gone back to Big Timber. We're safe here for a few days.'

Gus grabbed the collar of Harvey Goode's shirt and dragged him towards the door. The sounds of the injured cowboy's suffering could still be heard after he'd been pulled outside and the door reclosed. A gunshot, its usual sharp sound somehow dulled by the falling snow, reached those inside the cabin a minute later.

Dean Ridgeway struggled to his feet and crossed to the window. The man with the patch over his eye was making his way back to the cabin, nonchalantly replacing the spent bullet in his revolver's chamber, tossing aside the empty case into the deepening snow. Behind him lay the spread-eagled body of Harvey Goode, spatters of his blood leaving dark scars in the pure white snow.

'Laudanum,' Choctaw Jennings said, interrupting Dean's dark thoughts. 'Our friend could use some to ease his pain.'

Dean glowered at the outlaw, repulsed by the idea that he was expected to administer to their wounded man when his own patient had been cruelly disposed of like a mad dog. But he said nothing, the expression in the other man's face gave a clear indication that he was trying to help Dean. The message couldn't be clearer: be useful or be killed.

'There isn't much,' Dean said, 'and I don't know about dosage.' He looked at the big man lying on the bed and was shocked at the sight of the dried blood around his mouth. 'I was using laudanum to ease Harv's pain,' he went on, 'it might be the wrong thing to give him. I'm not a doctor. I don't know anything about these things.'

Choctaw gazed steadily at the young cowboy once more.

'If it eases his pain, it's the best we can hope for.'

But if it was wrong and the man died, thought Dean, he would be the one they blamed. Then, facing up to the situation, he knew that no matter what happened to the wounded man, they would kill him before they quit the shack. He crossed the room to reach for the small bottle on a high shelf. He poured some on to a spoon, told Choctaw that that was the dose he'd given Harv, then put it to Frank Felton's lips.

The outlaw leader had his eyes closed but his face was a continuous rhythm of tics and twitches, signifying his discomfort but confirming that he was still alive. Choctaw spoke to him, tried to lift his head and shoulders to get the medicine into his mouth. It wasn't easy. Choctaw undid the buttons on the long coat that Frank still wore. When it fell open Dean caught a glimpse of the bloodied shirt below. Frank moaned and the spoon was pushed into his mouth. Startled, he opened his eyes and his look fell instantly on the strange face of Dean Ridgeway. But Choctaw spoke quickly, reassuring Frank that he was still among friends.

'Take it down, Frank,' he said. 'It's medicine.'

Frank was suspicious 'Are you poisoning me, Choctaw?'

'It's laudanum, Frank. It'll take away the pain and help you sleep. We'll stay here until you're well enough to travel again. We're safe here.'

'Says who?' Frank's voice was faint.

'It's still snowing. No one's coming up here until that stops, which is likely to be days.'

Frank closed his eyes as though trying to assemble an argument, but they didn't re-open and he drifted off to sleep.

*

An hour later, after they'd eaten, the snow stopped falling. Dean looked out of the window to where Harvey Goode's body lay, almost completely covered. He wondered if there would be an opportunity to escape but he knew that even if there was he was likely to perish on the mountain. Jim Braddock was his ace in the hole; the outlaws believed that Harv had been his partner and weren't expecting anyone else to turn up. But he didn't know where Jim was, nor why he hadn't yet got back to the cabin. He'd expected him to arrive a long time ago but he supposed it had become necessary for him to find some shelter when the snowstorm was at its height. Of course, he didn't want him to return only to become another prisoner. He needed to contrive a warning but that wouldn't be easy. He was under constant scrutiny. Perhaps Jim would see Harv's body.

Thirty minutes passed before a chance presented itself; it came from an unlikely quarter. Gus Phipps had been standing over Frank Felton and the other two outlaws were curious as to what thoughts were passing through his head. Suddenly, he spoke to Dean, told him to get the mackinaw off Harv's body because he didn't need it any more and Frank was looking cold.

Choctaw and Drum regarded their companion with suspicion but said nothing. Whatever scheme Gus was hatching would become obvious soon enough.

'Don't get any ideas,' he told Dean as he opened the door.

Dean didn't mean to make a run for it but perhaps he could prepare that signal for Jim by leaving Harv's body in a position where he would be sure to be seen. He donned his heavy coat and went outside. When he reached the body he stopped and looked back to the cabin. He could see Gus through the partly opened door. He was not looking at Dean, he seemed to be deep in conversation with Choctaw and Drum.

'Frank's dead,' Gus was saying, pulling the long-barrelled Colt from its holster, 'so that cowboy is no longer needed. Now that the snow has stopped we can pick this cabin clean of provisions and get out of here. Nothing to hang around for.' He looked along the barrel and pulled the trigger.

Dean had just begun to bend to remove the coat when the bullet struck his head and pitched him forward across Harv's body.

SIX

Zeb Walters didn't know how long he'd been face down on the ground, but when his eyes opened neither the hour of the day nor the day of the week held significance for him. Existence consisted of an immense force that pinned him down, and an all-encompassing pain that was intensified by the slightest movement. For a long time he drifted in and out of consciousness, all physical and mental effort governed by his torment. One conscious moment brought with it the knowledge that he was dying. The realization didn't frighten him, it supplied an explanation for his nose being in the dirt, his eyes seeing nothing but blades of winter grass and the strange whistling sound that seemed to be coming from his chest as an accompaniment to his breathing. He closed his eyes, certain that his last breath would soon be exhaled.

Only a moment later the expectation of death was

replaced by an overwhelming compulsion to get to his feet. There was a message to deliver and although he couldn't recall its content, awareness of its importance filled his mind. He'd vowed to reach the Red Hammer ranch and was determined to succeed. It took a superhuman effort to raise himself but the agonies that had engulfed his mind and body were now replaced by an unworldly numbness. Nor was he deterred by the sight of dark bloodstains on the front of his coat and on the ground where he'd lain. He raised his head from the ground, grunted, then twisted his body to the left. Eyes were watching him, big brown eyes in a long face with a white blaze. The horse waited with patient curiosity while Zeb crawled towards him. It took a long time, but eventually, with the use of a stirrup leather, Zeb pulled himself upright and clambered on to the saddle. Of its own accord the horse set off on a downhill route to the ranch.

Consciousness deserted Zeb more than once on the journey to Red Hammer but, despite being draped over its neck, he was still clinging to the beast, when he was spotted by a couple of ranch hands two miles from the ranch house. In the yard, he was propped against a post of the horse corral and Charlie Grisham was summoned to the scene.

'It's Zeb,' somebody informed him.

'Shouldn't he be up at Fetterman's Pool?'

'He's been shot,' one of the hands who was bending over the wounded man told him.

'In the back,' somebody else added. That put a

bad taste in everyone's mouth. Nobody liked a killing although sometimes it was necessary, but there was no excuse for shooting a man in the back. Zeb Walters didn't deserve that; sometimes he was moody but never aggressive, just a cowhand doing a tough job.

'Has he said anything?' Charlie Grisham asked.

'No. He was unconscious when we found him. I don't know how he's managed to get all the way here in that condition.'

'Zeb,' the rancher said, 'it's Charlie Grisham. What happened? Who did this to you?'

Zeb's eyes remained closed, his head lolled to the right and there was barely a movement of his chest to signify that he was still breathing.

'Let's get him on to a bunk,' ordered Charlie.

Pat Hunt, who had taken charge of the wounded man when they'd got him off his horse, looked at his boss and shook his head. He pulled aside Zeb's coat to expose the ugly exit hole in his chest.

'Damnation,' muttered Charlie. 'Somebody get some water. We need to know who did this.'

A damp cloth was rubbed over Zeb's brow, then his lips were moistened. His eyelids flickered and for a moment he tried to focus on the nearest face.

'What happened, Zeb?' Charlie Grisham asked. Zeb's eyes closed again as though the lids were as heavy as farriers' hammers. 'It's Charlie, Zeb. You're safe here.'

Again, Zeb opened his eyes and this time there

seemed to be some determination to keep them open.

'You're back at the ranch, Zeb. Can you tell us what happened? Who shot you?'

To Zeb the world was now a hazy place; he had to concentrate on the voice and the face in front of him. *It's Charlie* were the words that he clung to. He'd made it with the message, he'd fulfilled the task he'd vowed to do. At last he'd achieved something of which Alice and Jane could be proud, something that perhaps atoned for the wrong he'd done, something that made him no less a man than. . .

'Who was it, Zeb?' urged Charlie Grisham.

The name 'Jim Braddock . . .' slipped out with Zeb's last breath.

Charlie Grisham was no stranger to acts of violence; one way or another they had peppered his life. Although they had soon lost the ability to shock him or even arouse in him anything more than the mildest interest when he was not directly affected by their commission, he was, in other circumstances, a man prepared to confront savagery with savagery. This killing demanded his intercession; Zeb Walters had been killed while on the Red Hammer payroll and perhaps because he was protecting Red Hammer stock. If so, he, Charlie Grisham, would want retribution against those who would steal from him; if he did not, the rest of the crew would still want his killer punished and would look to him for leadership.

'Jim Braddock.' When he repeated Zeb's words to Pat Hunt he spoke them aloud so that the other men gathered around were aware of the name that had been uttered.

'He works for the Broken Arrow,' Pat told his boss.

'I know who he is,' snapped Charlie. 'Just didn't strike me as a back-shooter.'

There were nods and grunts of agreement among the ranch hands.

Charlie picked out a couple of men and told them to get Zeb's body into the store shed.

'Pat,' he added, 'you'd better ride into Big Timber and tell the sheriff what's happened. He'll need to investigate the matter.'

'Sheriff's out with a posse looking for the killers of Dan Brix,' Pat Hunt replied.

Among the men a voice spoke. 'We don't have to go hunting for Zeb's killer. We know where he is. If we wait around for the sheriff Jim Braddock might flee the territory.'

'Hold on a minute,' Charlie Grisham said, giving himself time to think. He considered himself a good judge of men and he'd always assessed Jim Braddock as one of the best on the Broken Arrow; not only that, but the wrangling that had gone on over the years between himself and Hec Ridgeway had at last settled into a grudging friendliness. He didn't want to rekindle past differences by riding on to the Broken Arrow range with unproven accusations against one of their top men.

74

As though listening to Charlie's thoughts the man spoke again.

'There was bad blood between them,' he said.

Charlie raised his head to identify the speaker, a man called Judd Quarterstaff. Other men among his crew wore expressions that seemed to confirm Judd's words.

'Bad blood?'

'There was a card game in The Garter,' Judd told him. 'Jim Braddock cheated and Zeb lost all his money – although,' he added, 'the problem might have had more to do with a woman than money.'

'Nobody knows that,' Pat Hunt said, 'that's just whiskey talk.'

Judd Quarterstaff cast a glance in the direction of the body which was being carried across the yard to the cold outhouse.

'Looks like more than talk,' he said, the gruffness of his tone giving an indication of his reluctance to have anyone throw doubt on his views. 'Zeb's dead, isn't he?'

A question had been lurking in Charlie Grisham mind, now it came to the fore.

'Wasn't Zeb riding the line in the northern quarter?'

'That's right,' Pat Hunt agreed, 'him and young Harv Goode.'

'Then what was he doing down here?'

'Perhaps we should send someone up to the top cabin to question Harv.'

'Perhaps we should all go up in the morning,'

suggested Judd Quarterstaff, 'or ride over to Broken Arrow now and give Jim Braddock the justice he deserves.'

Men shuffled their feet; much as they disliked what had happened to Zeb it was up to the Red Hammer boss to decide how the matter was settled.

Someone shouted that a rider was approaching, but when everyone looked to the gateway it was a riderless horse that they saw. It was caught and brought to the place where the men were gathered, where a grim discovery was made.

'This is Harvey's horse,' said the handler, 'and there's blood on the saddle.'

There was a moment's silence, then Judd's gruff voice sounded.

'Jim Braddock's killed both of them.'

Pat Hunt spoke up. 'Perhaps I should organize a search,' he suggested.

Charlie Grisham's response: 'It'll soon be too dark,' was a thought spoken aloud. He was neither unaware nor uncaring of the fact that young Harvey Goode might be lying wounded somewhere between the ranch and the distant line cabin, but he didn't want to risk the safety of the other men in his employ who might pass within yards of their stricken companion without seeing him.

'There was snow in the hills today, boss,' Pat argued. 'We've got to look for him, can't leave him to freeze if he's still alive.'

'Take three men,' the boss told him, 'but I don't want you going into the high ground. Use your judgement and return when it becomes too dark to continue the search.'

Charlie Grisham was still reluctant to take any action that would cause a rift with Hec Ridgeway. The argument between Zeb and Jim Braddock had been a private affair, nothing to do with the ranch, so there was no reason for pursuing a course of action that could escalate into a range war. If Ben Stone hadn't been abroad chasing Frank Felton and his gang the matter could have been put into his hands, but he knew that he wouldn't be able to persuade his men to await the return of the sheriff now that there was the possibility that a second man had been killed. Judd Quarterstaff's latest words had had an effect on the men. Some, though not all, were making noises that signified agreement with the gruff cowhand's insistence on revenge.

He tried to defuse the growing unrest by introducing a topic that would evoke a degree of reverence among the cowboys.

'I guess I'll have to ride over to pass the news on to Zeb's wife and daughter.' It was a rare thing for a ranch hand to have such family attachments and Charlie Grisham's reference to grieving females had, for the most part, the effect on the men that he had hoped for. They shuffled their feet, bowed their heads and a couple even removed their hats, as though Alice Walters and her daughter Jane had suddenly joined their congregation. Charlie himself was contemplating taking his own daughter with him when he made the call on the widow, as she was a particular friend of Jane Walters.

Judd Quarterstaff, however, was tenacious. Times were changing and people were turning more and more to law officers to settle disputes, but that wasn't his way. He'd always ridden for outfits that made their own rules and fought their own fights. A crew had to have revenge for killings and their boss needed to lead them.

'What about Jim Braddock?' he asked.

'In the morning I'll ride over to the Broken Arrow, talk to Hec Ridgeway and hear what Jim Braddock has to say in his defence.'

'Jim Braddock isn't at the ranch,' someone informed the boss. 'Broken Arrow have a line cabin a few miles the other side of Fetterman's Pool. Jim's been riding the line up there for a few weeks now.'

The implication that Zeb had ridden so far with such an awful wound riled some of the men and they watched as Pat Hunt and the search crew prepared to ride away from the ranch yard. Charlie Grisham stopped them and issued fresh orders.

'Wait until I return from speaking to Zeb's widow, then every man who wants to help find Harv can come with us. Make sure they are all properly prepared. It'll be cold among those hills and we won't be travelling quickly until we find the lad.'

Alice Walters stood in the doorway of the small timber house that had been her home since arriving in Big Timber eight years earlier. A step behind her stood the slim figure of her daughter, Jane, who was holding a cocked revolver at her side, hidden from sight among the folds of her long skirt. The rumble of the approaching wagon had interrupted their evening meal and they had reacted guardedly to the male voice that had called to them from without.

'It's Charlie Grisham,' the voice had declared, so, apprehensively, they'd gone to the door. Alice's curiosity was heavy with foreboding; her husband's employer had never had reason to call at the house before. Charlie and his daughter sat astride their mounts behind a long buckboard. The two men on its high seat barely turned their heads to acknowledge the women at the door; they gazed straight ahead in order to convey the fact that it was the bundle on the long, flat wagon that needed their attention. By the time Alice and Jane had reached the back of the wagon Charlie and Annie Grisham had climbed down from their mounts and were at her side.

'I'm sorry,' Charlie Grisham said. He pulled aside the top of the tarpaulin that covered the body in the wagon, revealing the face of Alice's dead husband.

Later, when the initial impact of the death of husband and father had been absorbed by the Walters women and the body had been taken on to the undertaker in Big Timber, the Red Hammer boss imparted the little information he had. They were sitting around the table, the two daughters side by side with Charlie Grisham and Alice Walters opposite.

'And you are sure it was Jim Braddock?' Alice

said. 'I wouldn't have taken him for the gunfighting type.'

'We know there had been trouble between them recently. Zeb claimed he'd been cheated by Jim. We can only assume that that was the incident that led to the killing.'

Jane Walters dried her eyes on a soft linen handkerchief. She wasn't unaware of the flare-up in the Garter that had caused her father to be locked up overnight, nor was she unaware of the gossip that had followed. For several days little else had been talked about in the store where she worked and she'd been angered and embarrassed by the easy manner in which her mother's character had been blackened by their neighbours. However, the pain she experienced from their overheard remarks went deeper than resentment on her mother's behalf. A greater concern was the fear that their vile comments were true.

As a settlement, Big Timber was growing but, in Jane's opinion, the increasing population was still devoid of suitable bachelors from which a girl could choose a husband. Although he was unaware of her regard for him, Jim Braddock was lodged in her mind as the best man in town. He was older than she, it was true, but that was often the case in these under-populated areas. In his favour, it seemed to her that he was polite, helpful, strong and good-looking. No one had a bad word to say about him and she had never heard him curse or seen him spit. Those restraints, she'd convinced herself, were a mark of respect for her, placed upon himself only when he was in her presence. Schemes for attracting his attention had begun to develop in her mind, something more than the smiles and side-glances whenever she saw him in town, but the gossip that linked him with her mother had changed all that. She felt betrayed, rejected in preference for her own mother, and the hurt had curdled inside her for several weeks.

'I suppose he denies it,' she said.

'We haven't spoken to him. It's possible he's up at the Broken Arrow line cabin near Fetterman's Pool. I'll be leading a party up there to arrest him but there is another man missing. Young Harvey Goode was with your father and his horse has come back to the ranch with blood on the saddle. We need to look for Harvey in case he's lying hurt somewhere on the hillside.'

'Then you'll get Jim Braddock?'

'It would be better if the sheriff arrested him.' Charlie was still reluctant to take matters into his own hands especially if meant riding on to the Broken Arrow range. Hec Ridgeway wouldn't let that happen without repercussions.

'The sheriff is out of town,' Jane said with the same sort of aggression that Judd Quarterstaff had shown earlier.

'We'll do what we can,' Charlie said, hoping to appease the women without making any promises.

Jane Walters placed on the table the gun she'd been holding since the sound of the rattling wagon had first interrupted their meal.

'I'm coming with you,' she declared.

'That's not a good idea,' Charlie told her. 'It'll be hard riding. There's no place for a girl in a group like that.'

'He killed my father,' she replied. 'I want to see justice done.'

SEVEN

The cave recommended by Jim Braddock as a place of shelter was almost two hundred feet above the spot where the girl and the old man had dug themselves into the snow. Under normal conditions they would have made the ascent in a few minutes but the weather had deteriorated to a near blizzard, turning the uphill trek into an arduous undertaking made more difficult by the girl's stubbornness.

Jim had told the girl to ride her pony while he shared his horse with the old man so that he could hold him securely in the saddle, but the girl had refused, had insisted on transporting the old man on the travois that had been used as the foundation of the structure in which they'd gone to earth. At first Jim Braddock had argued, insisting that they would all be frozen before they could get the contraption harnessed to the pony, but the girl had ignored him, setting about the task with uncovered hands.

'We haven't got time for this,' Jim had yelled at

her through the wind-blown snow, but she'd merely turned away from him, shrugged the blanket so that it dislodged the snow that was piling on her shoulders, then bent to the task of securing the long poles of the travois to the primitive horse trappings.

Jim Braddock was about to repeat his exhortations but instead his attention was attracted to the old man, who was lying on the travois. His eyes were now open, they were black, surprisingly bright, and fixed on Jim's face. They showed neither fear nor pain, but a depth of understanding that unnerved Jim. The Sioux's face was small and lined with a thousand wrinkles that even creased his nose. If he was dying, and that was the supposition uppermost in Jim's mind, he was doing so with a calmness that reflected contentment with all he'd achieved in life, an acceptance that his time had come to leave this world. There was also an expression of pride, but that, Jim suspected, was for the girl who was refusing to submit to a white man's orders. For Jim there seemed to be a special message: not to hinder the girl and all would be well.

For a moment he studied the slight form working at the pony, her back to him, the blanket that covered her head and shoulders heavy with snow. She moved as though unaffected by the cold but her hands and bare legs were almost blue against the whiteness of the falling snow. Her ankle-high moccasins were almost lost from sight. These people were no different from himself, Jim thought; the winter had come earlier than expected for them, too. He admired her fortitude but remained concerned for her well-being. He hoped that among the items in the pack she'd loaded on her horse there was some warmer clothing. Argument, he knew, was the last thing that was needed at this time. They needed to get out of the snowstorm quickly and, although that was not going to be achieved by using the travois, he reckoned that any delay would be halved if he helped instead of arguing.

They didn't speak; indeed the girl didn't even acknowledge his assistance when he began to attach the second pole to the other side of the pony, but kept her head bent so that all he saw was the blanket covering it, but there was a sense of togetherness when they eventually began the uphill climb to their destination. Jim walked at the head of the Indian pony, guiding the way, head down, barely able to see more than a couple of steps ahead. The girl, leading Jim's horse, walked at the side of the travois to ensure the old man's comfort.

A smell hung about the cave that the horses didn't like. Jim wondered if it was the lair of a hibernating bear, but a quick exploration proved that it was empty. He carried the old man inside while the girl dragged the unharnessed travois to the very back of the cave. The old man was wrapped in a bearskin and there were other stretched skins and woollen blankets on the travois. Jim urged the girl to take one for her own warmth, but she used them to make a resting place for the old man. There was an abundance of dry twigs scattered around the cave that had been blown in or carried in by prowling animals. Jim gathered some and built a fire, leaving the girl free to settle the old man on the rudimentary bed. He was aware that she watched him, cast curious glances as though humiliated by the assistance he was giving. However, they were all grateful when flames began to catch the larger twigs.

Thoughts of Dean Ridgeway back at the cabin with the injured Harvey Goode flooded into Jim's mind. He knew that it behoved him to get back there as soon as possible and he hoped that there would be a let-up in the snowfall that would enable him to leave. He went to the mouth of the cave and looked out on to the bleak landscape. Overhead the sky was grey and snow was falling in large flakes. There was no prospect of an early departure.

He unsaddled his horse and rubbed the water out of its coat with a handful of twigs. Before doing the same to the pony he threw a look at the girl. There had been little indication that a truce existed between them and he wasn't sure she would want him to groom her horse. There had been fire in her eyes when he'd first seen her and although they had toiled in unison to get to the shelter of the cave, Jim was sure that her animosity would resurface if his behaviour gave her cause for suspicion. But at the moment she had her back to him, was talking quietly to the old man, so he gave the pony a little attention.

Later, when the fire had warmed the cave and the

old man had fallen asleep, Jim approached the girl. He saw her hand rest on the rifle, a sign that she didn't trust him and that she wouldn't be afraid to use it if it became necessary to do so.

'My name's Jim,' he said. 'What's yours?'

'I am Waktaya,' she said after a moment, 'The One Who Guards.' Her hand gripped the barrel of the rifle as if to emphasize the meaning.

'How did you get separated from the rest of your band?' Jim figured they'd been left behind because the old man was too ill to survive a nomadic life in winter, and the band, knowing they were being pursued, would expect the pair to be found by the soldiers and returned to the reservation.

The girl, however, was clearly confused by the question and her brow puckered in a small frown before she replied:

'There is no one else.'

'No one else,' repeated Jim Braddock, then he asked, 'Aren't you part of the group that left the reservation with Grey Eagle?'

Waktaya looked at the sleeping figure beside her.

'This is Grey Eagle of the Hunkpapa Sioux,' she announced.

Jim looked at the pair with astonishment.

'You mean you've come all the way from Pine Ridge alone? With only one horse?'

'We had another horse but it went lame five days ago.'

'What are you doing here?' Jim wanted to know.

'Grey Eagle has returned to the land where he

became a warrior. This is where he has chosen to die.'

'He's come all this way to die?' Jim Braddock was incredulous. 'The army think he's planning to renew hostilities. There have been attacks on farms that are being blamed on Grey Eagle and his followers. They are the markers by which the soldiers are following you.'

Momentarily the girl's face registered alarm. Jim Braddock assumed it had been stirred by her learning that she and Grey Eagle were being pursued by soldiers, but when she spoke it was in defence of the farm raids along the route.

'We were hungry,' she told Jim. 'I stole some eggs. Once I killed a chicken.' The smile that touched Jim's face only served to anger Waktaya. 'You think it is funny that we were starving?'

'No,' he said. 'I think it is funny that a little farmyard stealing has the army fearful of a Sioux uprising. Grey Eagle must have been a formidable opponent.'

Waktaya's head lifted a little, a sign of pride.

'Yes,' she said. 'My grandfather has many scalps.'

'I'm sure he's as proud of you as you are of him,' Jim told her. 'Not many people would have undertaken this journey.' By Jim's reckoning the journey had to be at least three hundred miles.

'Who else should do it?' she asked. 'I am the last of his family.'

'Even so, it wasn't without danger.'

'My grandfather dreamed and it removed all fear.

Wakatanka, the Great Spirit, travelled with us. Grey Eagle would not die until he'd reached his chosen place.' She paused a moment, looked at the figure asleep beside her. 'We are here,' she said. 'He will not see the sun go down.'

Jim Braddock studied Waktaya. Never before had he seen anyone capable of displaying so much ferocity and then so much serenity in such a short space of time. She had a longish face, emphasized by the distinctive high cheekbones of her people. Her dark eyes reduced to narrow slits when she was angry but were wondrous large when, as now, her mood was gentle.

A surge of unexpected jealousy swamped Jim's senses; his was a history of a cowboy's loneliness: it was all he had known. No one had ever looked at him in such a manner – and never would. Loyalty and respect were both evident in her expression but there was also something much deeper and warmer: love, Jim supposed, and he found it necessary to wipe his arm across his mouth to distract himself from the thoughts in his head.

'Who told you that there were soldiers chasing us?' Waktaya suddenly asked.

'I met a cavalry patrol earlier,' Jim replied. 'They'll take you back to Pine Ridge.'

Before he'd finished speaking the girl had moved with a suddenness that startled Jim. She'd snatched up the rifle and held it with violent intent. Fierceness flashed in her eyes, the flames of the fire reflecting in them adding a devilish aspect to her countenance.

'I will not go with soldiers,' she hissed. 'I will kill them if they try to touch me again.' She swung the rifle until it was pointing at Jim's chest. 'I will kill anyone who tries to touch me.'

Jim raised his hands in placatory fashion.

'I'm not going to hurt you,' he told her, but such was the vehemence of her expression that Jim wasn't at all sure that his words had any meaning for her.

A noise like a cough, guttural but soft, turned their attention to the old man. His eyes were open and fixed on Jim Braddock. He spoke again, nothing more than a single word that drew his granddaughter to his side. She bent down to him, placing the rifle on the ground while she spoke soft words of solace to him. Jim turned away, diplomatically returning to his post at the mouth of the cave.

The snow was falling with less intensity. Soon, Jim figured, he would be able to quit the shelter of the cave and get back to the cabin. He'd hardly spared a thought for Dean Ridgeway and Harvey Goode since coming across the Sioux couple; he was probably as much needed there as he was here. Indeed, the girl was a great deal more competent than his boss's son in almost every respect.

He looked back into the far reaches of the cave where Waktaya was kneeling at her grandfather's side. She had done little to ameliorate her own discomfort, but the blanket around the upper part of her body was slowly drying in the warmth created by the small fire. Her legs remained bare but she hadn't shown any sign that she was suffering from their being cold. Jim almost smiled as the thought crossed his mind that she had no need of outer warmth because she clearly had a fire – an inferno – burning inside her. But he didn't smile, instead he wondered what tragedy had occurred in her young life to have left her with such vehement hatred of Americans. It added another layer to her courage: travelling so far with an old, dying man when she expected nothing but a threat to her own safety from those she met on the way.

Several minutes later, while he was talking to and stroking the horses, he heard the first low notes of a melody. The girl was singing: amusing her grandfather, Jim supposed, in the weariness of his infirmity. Only when her voice began to rise did the mournfulness of her singing become apparent; her keening was a dirge.

Waktaya ignored the American when he reached her side and continued her song even while she prepared her grandfather for the world beyond. Her prediction that he would not see the sun go down had come true. From among her chattels she produced an ointment which she rubbed into the dead man's skin, rendering him as white as the snow beyond the entrance of the cave. She placed three eagle feathers and a stone axe in his folded hands: symbols of wisdom and war, then she wrapped him tightly in the blanket on which he was lying. Jim's hand's were brushed aside when he tried to help, and moments later, when it was apparent that she meant to use the great bear robe as a shroud, his protest was greeted with a scornful look.

'You need to wrap that around yourself,' he told her. 'His winters will no longer be as cold as yours.'

'My grandfather's coat was known to all the people of the village he left behind,' she told him. 'It will identify him in the village he is going to.'

She had told him that her name meant The One Who Guards, but if she had earned it for her care of Grey Eagle, then that was a duty duly dispensed. There was nothing more she could do for him; she needed to consider her own safety, but perhaps, he figured, he was treading into the territory of her religion where he had no right to interfere. He watched as she used a long bone needle to stitch together the edges of the robe. It wasn't an easy task but when it was completed the cadaver was completely enclosed. It was a gesture, Jim guessed, to emphasize her determination in the matter. So tough had it been to force the needle through the thick coat that she had been left with bleeding fingers. It increased Jim's appreciation of her mettle but did nothing to ease his concern. The long journey back to Pine Ridge would be more arduous if the winter conditions persisted, there was little chance of survival if she continued to disregard her own well-being.

Snow was no longer falling when her ministrations were completed. Jim Braddock could no longer delay his return to the line cabin but he was curious about Waktaya's plans.

'There are holy grounds near here. Grey Eagle chose them as his last resting place. I will take him there.'

Jim Braddock knew the place she referred to; they were called burial grounds by the Sioux but no one had ever been put in the ground there. The shrouded corpses had been lifted on to platforms and left to decay with the passage of time. It had been many years since the body of the last Sioux warrior had been offered to the elements at that place, yet still there were hidebound mounds atop long-legged platforms. How the slight girl standing before him proposed to hoist her dead grandfather on to such a structure defied reason.

'The travois always had another purpose,' she told him, explaining her determination not to abandon it in the snow.

'Even so,' said Jim, 'even if, despite this unexpected snow, you were able to erect the platform, you wouldn't be able to get him up there on your own.'

The girl's reply surprised him. 'Grey Eagle travelled in the belief that all would be well, that Wakantanka would provide me with assistance. Before he died he told me that you were the one sent by the Great Spirit.'

The protest that Jim knew should have been his immediate response never passed his lips. He wasn't sure why he couldn't refuse to help but he did know that he couldn't abandon the girl to a Herculean task that he knew she would tackle with or without him. Clearly, she was involving him because of a promise she'd made to her dying grandfather, but she couldn't disguise her distrust. Once again the rifle was in her hands and her eyes watched warily every move he made.

'There's an injured man back at my cabin,' he told her. 'I must get back there as quickly as possible.'

With the girl astride the pony and the travois hitched behind, Jim led the way to the burial site. Before leaving he had thrown a long blanket over the girl's lap which reached down to cover her bare legs. Waktaya had been both surprised by and suspicious of the act, but after that he had ignored her and she saw nothing but his back on the short journey to the Sioux holy ground.

Converting the travois into a funeral platform proved a simple operation for Waktaya. Even cold and ankle-deep in snow, she worked adroitly and completed the task swiftly. Fixing the legs securely into the ground was the most difficult part of the job, but the small shovel Jim carried behind his saddle for rescuing trapped beeves came in handy for hole-digging, too. The finished structure wasn't as high as many of the others, which did not please the girl, but which proved a boon when it came time to raise the body. They used ropes and the horses to hoist the body. It was an inelegant but effective procedure.

'Come back to the cabin with me,' Jim invited. 'It

will be warmer there and I'll give you some food for the journey home.'

He was surprised when she didn't refuse.

'I know a little bit about medicines,' she said, keeping her eyes averted, talking as though her reason for staying with him was because she had a debt to repay. 'Perhaps I can help your injured friend.'

EIGHT

They rode in silence, the girl to the left of Braddock and half a length behind. From time to time the cowboy twisted in the saddle to check that the Sioux girl was still with him. Since he had encountered her the overriding emotion she had displayed had been suspicion. Despite his assistance at the burial place and his efforts to protect her from the winter storm, he didn't think he'd chipped away even a small portion of the hard shell that encased her emotions. He wouldn't have been surprised if, wordlessly, she'd struck out on a different route, but every time he looked back she was there, her head covered and eyes lowered so that she seemed capable of seeing little more than the neck of her pony.

Her thoughts, he figured would be centred on the grandfather who had predicted his own death with such accuracy, so he was loath to interrupt her melancholy. Further attempts at conversation could keep until they'd gained the refuge of the line cabin. If she would permit it, he would help her to prepare for the return journey to Pine Ridge, although currently he had no idea what form that assistance would take.

At the back of his mind still lingered the notion of handing her over to the cavalry detail he'd encountered; they needed to be informed of the death of Grey Eagle to put an end to their patrol, but Waktaya's earlier reaction to the idea of contact with soldiers was still fresh in his mind. Her fear of them was genuine, the result, perhaps, of being in a village that had been devastated by military action. He doubted if he would ever learn the truth of the matter but he was reluctant to put her into a situation that caused her distress; he was still in awe of the devotion that had brought her on such a journey.

Later he concluded, when they'd had time to consider the ramifications of the eastbound journey, they would decide the best way to get her back to the reservation. He threw another glance behind. It seemed to him that he caught a slight movement of her head, as though she had averted her eyes, reluctant to let him know that she had been watching him.

Progress down the snow-covered hillside was slow. More than once his iron-shod mount slipped, instilling caution in both rider and horse. It prompted thoughts about the accident earlier in the day and, briefly, guilt nudged Jim's mind. Perhaps it had been a mistake to remain with the girl; his first duty was to the man who paid for his labour, but he'd done what seemed right at the time. Besides, Hec Ridgeway wanted his son to learn the rougher side of ranching and that wouldn't be achieved by holding his hand every step of the way. Dean had to learn that sometimes a man had to find his own answers to the problems that arose.

If Jim had remained at the cabin he could not have done more for Harvey Goode than he'd instructed Dean Ridgeway to do. It was simply a matter of keeping him alive until the Red Hammer outfit sent someone to evacuate the injured man back to the ranch. Jim's thoughts strayed to Zeb Walters and the progress of his mercy dash. Had he outrun the snow and reached the ranch, and was a crew already on its way to reach their injured comrade? Or had caution dictated their response and delayed their departure until the morning's new light?

A sudden unexpected sound interrupted his meditation. It was distant and distorted, muffled by the layer of snow, which was killing sounds that usually echoed in the air as they bounced off hard rock surfaces. It carried to Jim as little more than a pop, almost playful in its tone and abruptness, but he knew it had been a gunshot. More important, it had come from the direction of the line cabin, which was little more than a quarter of a mile ahead. He turned in the saddle to look at the girl.

It was clear that Waktaya, too, had heard and recognized the sound. She had stopped her pony and pushed the blanket away from her head as though anxious not to miss any subsequent noises that might be relevant to her own safety.

'It came from the direction of the cabin,' Jim told her calmly. 'It must be my partner. Perhaps there are wolves prowling around.' He had no idea what Dean could be shooting at but, to ease any anxiety that might be growing within the girl, he'd felt a need to offer a possible explanation. In fact, his speculation wasn't groundless; it was quite possible that hungry wolves had caught the scent of the cattle they'd herded up from the creek.

It was the likelihood of Dean Ridgeway in the role of protector that Jim had difficulty accepting. Never before had he shown himself capable of handling two tasks simultaneously and, having already been given the job of tending to the needs of Harvey Goode, it was unlikely that he would stray beyond the confines of the cabin. Jim shrugged; he would learn the reason for the gunshot when he got there. They moved on, slowly, Jim casting glances all around as he rode.

Their angle of approach brought them to a point above the rear eastern corner of the cabin. Smoke was rising in a peaceful curl from the stovepipe, which made Jim anticipate the hot coffee waiting within, but for a moment he paused, casting an eye over the small bunch of beeves that were milling around in the corral below. He couldn't detect any undue distress, no sign that they'd been disturbed by a predator. He gathered up the reins and pre-pared to guide his mount down to the crude timber building.

Unnoticed, Waktaya had pushed her pony alongside Jim's horse and now, silently, she reached out her right hand and rested it on the cowboy's left forearm. It was a gentle touch, virtually weightless but powerful enough to dissuade him from urging his horse forward. He turned to the girl, curious at her intervention, then transfixed by the almost mystical expression on her face. Her countenance showed none of those signs that inform the watcher of pleasure or pain; no smiles, no frowns. Across her facial bones her soft skin was taut but lustrous and unaffected by the icy chill. It was the very stillness of her features that transmitted the message that required attention. Her large, black eyes seemed to be gazing into another world, a place in which it was unsafe to travel without a friendly guide.

Jim Braddock wanted to question her, wanted her to tell him what she knew, but at that moment was wary of using words, afraid that talk would destroy her concentration and disperse the information she had already acquired. Although, to Jim, the lapse of time seemed almost endless, it was, in fact, a mere moment until Waktaya pointed to a place at the foot of the bank that was twenty yards from the front of the cabin.

Jim could see a snow-covered mound with an object that resembled a grey blanket tossed on top.

'What is it?' he wondered. 'Let's take a look.'

Waktaya, whose hand still rested on Jim's arm, pressed harder, a warning of danger although she couldn't specify its nature.

'I'll be careful,' he said, but before moving forward he surveyed the area again. There were three little buildings at the far side of the cabin: a privy, a work shed where they kept tools, wire and an assortment of implements necessary when isolated from the main ranch, and the small shelter that was used as a stable. Jim could see Dean Ridgeway's horse moving around inside and felt a tug of irritation that the young man hadn't fully closed the door to keep the animal warm. He figured that Dean's excuse would be that he'd been preoccupied with his patient and that care of his horse had slipped his mind. That was the kind of sloppy attitude Hec expected Jim to knock out of his son but, like shooting at wolves while caring for a sick man, handling two tasks at once again seemed to be beyond Dean's capabilities.

'There are horses,' Waktaya said as the high whinny of an unseen, disgruntled animal carried to them from the other side of the cabin.

Briefly, the thought occurred to Jim that Red Hammer had reacted more quickly than expected, but he soon dismissed that thought. Logic told him that a response in such a short space of time was impossible. The more likely caller was a Broken Arrow rider with a message from the boss. Such a visitor would have pleased Dean; he would have someone else to share the responsibility.

'Come on,' he said, 'let's see who has come a-calling.'

If Jim Braddock was relieved by the thought that

Dean Ridgeway had not been alone for the past few hours it was an emotion not shared by the Sioux girl. Although she released her hold on Jim's arm as though granting permission for him to go forward, her words kept him beside her on the bank.

'Something is wrong,' was all she said and she stretched out her arm again towards the snow-covered mound as though it held an explanation for all things.

The deep snow killed the sound of the horses as they walked down the incline, the riders swaying slightly with the exaggerated movement caused by the slow pace of the animals. By the time they reached the bottom of the slope they could see that there were four horses tethered to the hitching pole at the front of the line cabin. Jim's brow furrowed; he recognized none of the horses and none of them carried the brand mark of the Broken Arrow. The identities of his visitors were a mystery that added extra weight to Waktaya's warning of something being wrong.

They followed the line of the bank, a route which would bring them to the front of the cabin and close to the place where the grey mound bulged strangely in the flat whiteness. As they rode Jim's attention alternated between scrutinizing the mound and watching for activity within the cabin. He could see a timid light glowing beyond the cabin's small window but, for the moment, it appeared that their arrival had passed unnoticed by those within. The further they descended, however, the more his interest was captured by the shape at the foot of the incline. The material he could see was unexpectedly familiar. The moment that he recognized Dean Ridgeway's clothing coincided with the perception that the form he was observing had arms and legs, that it was a man face down in the snow, not a discarded blanket.

Careless of any scrutiny from the cabin, Jim dismounted and knelt by the body of the heir to the Broken Arrow ranch. He lifted the young man's head and saw that blood still seeped from a forehead wound. It was a sign that he wasn't yet dead, so Jim gripped his shoulders in an effort to turn him and inspect the injury more closely. The bullet had not gone into his head. Instead, it had gouged in his brow a three-inch trail that disappeared into the hairline. A low moan escaped the wounded man, confirming that he was still alive, but Jim's attention was now focused elsewhere. Shifting the wounded man had uncovered what lay beneath, had revealed the cause of the lump that Dean's body had been draped over.

It took only a brief glimpse for Jim to know that there was no hope of resuscitation for the Red Hammer rider. In death, Harvey Goode's face reflected the torment he had known in his final moments. His mouth was open in a silent scream and his eyes were large, bulging in their sockets.

Jim threw a glance over his shoulder towards the cabin, wondering at the identities of the men within, then he turned his attention to the girl on the pony.

'Ride, Waktaya,' he told her. 'Get away from here.'

Waktaya regarded the bodies in the snow, her face betraying no emotion, prompting in Jim Braddock the belief that she was not unaccustomed to such gruesome scenes.

'Go,' he insisted, and began the struggle to lift Dean Ridgeway off the ground. For the present there was nothing he could do for Harvey Goode; his body had to freeze under the snow but he meant to hoist Dean on to his horse and get clear of the cabin as quickly as possible. If he was discovered he would be at the mercy of those within the cabin.

Lifting Dean wasn't an easy task. He was a big lad and, being unconscious, a dead weight. The conditions underfoot added an extra and substantial handicap to the job. Riding boots were all well and good when astride a horse but were a hazard when walking in snowy and icy conditions. More than once Jim slipped, usually losing all the progress he'd made in trying to get Dean into an upright position. It was on the second occasion, when he'd hit the ground hard and uttered a rough oath in frustration, that he realized that the Sioux girl was still near at hand. The blanket in which she'd been swaddled had been discarded, was gathered in front of her across the pony. She sat erect in her buckskin dress, her eyes fixed with vigilance on the cabin. In her hands she held the rifle with which she had threatened Jim only hours earlier.

'I told you to go,' Jim snapped at her. 'The people in there are killers. There's no reason to put yourself in danger. Go.'

In imperious manner the girl turned her head slightly in his direction.

'I am Waktaya,' she said, 'The One Who Guards.' There was a solemnity to her words that defied objection, a stateliness that demanded recognition. In that moment it seemed to Jim that the girl was announcing herself as a warrior, that she had attained a position she would never relinquish, that she could match his nobleness. If he was prepared to die to rescue his friend then she, too, was prepared to die.

He dismissed the notion that he was doing anything noble; he was merely doing what Hec Ridgeway paid him to do: protecting his property. He wasn't anxious to die for anyone. He didn't want Waktaya to die either, so, as the best solution was to get away from this place as quickly as possible, he didn't argue, he merely bent, grabbed Dean under the arms and hauled him to his feet. In Jim's opinion the girl's determination was misplaced. An old Hall single-shot wouldn't deter the men in the cabin. They were killers and would emerge with guns blazing if they became aware of the presence of Waktaya and himself.

They almost got away undetected. Jim was grateful for the dimming light and the cold; the approaching darkness provided a little cover while he endeavoured to get Dean on to the horse, and he figured the cold was keeping the killers clustered around the well-fuelled stove and away from the window. But a stumble and a collision with his horse betrayed the covert activity just at the moment when success seemed achievable.

It was the boots, of course, that caused the catastrophe. He had hoisted Dean on to his shoulder and was preparing to throw him over the saddle when his foot slipped. He didn't fall, nor did he drop Hec's son but, during his clumsy attempt to stay upright, he barged Dean's head against the shoulder of his horse with sudden force. Already skittish because of the frozen ground, the horse slithered and broadcast its nervousness with a sharp whinny.

Jim cursed but, as happens in times of crisis, he reacted with unexpected speed and strength, launching Dean from his shoulder and across the saddle with unexpected accuracy. At the same moment he heard the report of Waktaya's rifle and turned his head towards the cabin. He didn't know if the result of her shot was the one she had intended but it gave them a few extra seconds to make their getaway.

A man, Drum Hayes, had emerged from the cabin, gun in hand, to investigate the disturbance. Waktaya's shot hadn't hit him. Instead, the bullet had hit the kerosene lantern that hung on a nail near the doorpost. It exploded, spreading oil and flame in all directions. Some of it landed on the man, burning his face and setting alight his shirt.

Drum yelled and stumbled back into the cabin without discharging his weapon, his hands busily beating at his clothing to stop the flames spreading. In his panic he collided with Gus Phipps, inadvertently blocking the doorway so that no one inside the building could get a clear shot at the newcomers.

Waktaya was busy with the Hall, working to replace the spent cartridge with a live round which she gripped between two fingers of her left hand. Jim shouted to her as he swung a leg over his mount and settled himself behind the saddle.

'Ride,' he yelled, 'and don't stop.' Shots followed them as they rode away but in the gloom even gunmen like Gus Phipps and Choctaw Jennings were unlikely to hit moving targets. They rode as quickly as conditions permitted, though Jim continually cast looks behind, certain that the killers would mount up and give chase. The snow-covered ground was not only a handicap against speed, it also left a trail that could be followed by a child.

They ran on for a mile, Jim hanging on to the seat of Dean's pants to make sure he didn't fall off, but he knew they couldn't travel like this for much longer. Not only was he slowed down because his horse was carrying double, but he was unsure what extra damage he was doing to Dean. Travelling head down in juddering fashion wasn't an aid to recovery. He looked behind but there was no immediate sign of pursuit.

Up ahead, Wakataya, who had opened up a gap

between them, had pulled her pony to a halt. Jim wasn't sure whether or not he was annoyed by her wilful disobedience.

'I told you to keep going,' he said when he reached her. There wasn't much rancour in his tone. She said nothing but her silence and the long look at the figure hanging head down across Jim's horse expressed eloquently her thoughts. They could not continue in this manner.

Jim voiced his regret that they hadn't been able to get Dean's horse from the little stable behind the cabin, but he had a plan in mind. They were heading in the direction of Fetterman's Pool; the creek where they'd met the Red Hammer riders was a little distance ahead. He explained his idea to Waktaya. It meant leaving her with the wounded man while he rode on to the creek with her pony in tow so that their pursuers would believe they were still together. When he got to the creek he would make it appear that they had ridden south along its bed, heading down towards Big Timber and the ranching communities. Instead, he would go north then circle back to rejoin her and Dean. If the killers were unable to find them then it was reasonable to assume that they would hightail it out of this country as quickly as possible. It was the belief that they wouldn't want a posse on their tail that reminded Jim of the conversation he'd had earlier that day with Harvey Goode. Perhaps the men at the cabin were those who had killed Deputy Brix and who were already being chased by Sheriff Stone's posse.

They found a suitable place where, by dismounting on to boulders so that they left no feet marks on the ground, Dean was unloaded and nestled in a niche where the Sioux girl would watch over him until Jim returned. The growing darkness would hide them from the pursuers and, wrapped in Waktaya's blankets, Jim was certain the young man would survive until they could get him back home.

He didn't tarry, time was essential and he wasn't sure how far behind the killers would be. He didn't want to be in their view when he reached the creek; everything depended upon him fooling them into believing their quarry was on the trail to Big Timber.

'I'll return as soon as possible,' he told the girl; then from the boulder he leapt into his saddle, gathered up the loose reins of the Sioux girl's pony and rode away into the closing night.

109

NINE

By the time he'd pushed aside Drum Hayes, who was stumbling, shouting and swatting at his burning clothes with windmilling arm movements, Gus Phipps was able to fire only two shots at the fleeing riders before conceding that anything more would be a waste of ammunition. Choctaw Jennings reached his side and fired a token shot, then asked,

'Who was that?'

'What does it matter who they were,' grunted the one-eyed outlaw, 'let's get after them.' Gus turned back into the cabin, needing to collect his coat before giving chase in the ice-cold night.

Drum Hayes, finally content that he was neither injured by the burning oil nor in danger of his clothes rekindling into flames, spoke against pursuit.

'What sense is there in giving chase?' he grumbled. 'You won't catch them.'

Choctaw was unconvinced. 'Their trail will be easy to follow. You can see hoofprints in the snow a mile ahead.'

'We can't let them get away,' chipped in Gus Phipps. 'They'll tell someone we're here. They could be with the posse.'

Drum Hayes, scoffing at the idea, taunted Gus:

'I reckon with one eye closed I would still be able to recognize an Indian girl. How many posses have you heard of that included a squaw?'

Choctaw, whose knowledge of the incident consisted of little more than a glimpse of two fleeing horsemen disappearing into the night-time gloom, looked to Gus for confirmation of Drum's words.

'Is that right, Gus, they were Indians? I didn't know there were any still living around here.'

'Who knows who lives in these wild places,' grumbled Gus, still eager to set off in pursuit.

'What do you think they were after?' Choctaw asked.

'A cow, probably.' Drum spoke with casual authority, as though his reading of the situation was indisputable. 'Looking for some meat to see them through the winter. No reason for them to be suspicious of an occupied cabin, and who are they going to tell if they are? They came raiding, which means they are as much wanted by the army as we are by the law.'

'What should we do?'

'Stick to our plan,' Drum said. 'Now that Frank is dead we'll head west, get across the border into Idaho and lie low there for a while.'

'I don't like it,' Gus Phipps said. 'We shouldn't let them ride away. We should make sure they don't talk to anyone.'

'They were going in the direction we've left behind,' Drum replied. 'We'd be wearying the horses for no reason. Forget about chasing them. We'll quit this place at first light.'

With Dean Ridgeway secure and warm in the nest that Waktaya had built for him after Jim Braddock's departure, she turned her attention to the wound in his brow. He had been lucky. He would have been killed if he had delayed bending to remove Harvey Goode's coat a moment longer. The bullet would have struck him between the eyes, entered his head and shattered his brain. Instead, it had caught only the top of his brow and the angle of travel had caused it to hit the hard frontal bone, which had deflected the lump of lead up and over the top of his head. All that the bullet had achieved was to render him unconscious and leave a gouge reminiscent of a blow from a Sioux war axe. Packing it with ice had stopped the bleeding and prevented it from swelling but it still looked black and ugly against the young man's ashen face.

Waktaya had worked anxiously, her senses keen for any indication that their pursuers were approaching. To a large degree the sound of hoofbeats would be muffled by the snow; the riders could be close before she heard them, so it was necessary to be vigilant while she worked, scan the trail that she and her charge had travelled to catch the earliest sight of them. When Jim had ridden off she'd expected them to be only moments away, but minutes had passed without any indication of pursuit.

Dean Ridgeway stirred, his eyes opened, then screwed closed when he moved his head. When he moaned, Waktaya rushed to his side.

'You must be quiet.' She spoke in a hushed tone. 'Horsemen are hunting for us.'

Dean regarded her with curiosity. 'Who are you?'

Her words didn't answer his enquiry, but she hoped they would have more meaning for the invalid.

'Jim will soon return. Until then you must be quiet.'

With consciousness returning, however, Dean began seeking answers to other questions; Waktaya provided none. Although she was now certain that no one from the cabin was following in their wake she was still uninclined to curtail her vigilance. In the past, enemies had attacked her village while it slept and she was determined that that would never happen to her again. The mere thought of it brought to her mind the tumult of thundering hoofbeats, bugle calls, shouts and gunfire, and she pictured the ugly faces of soldiers intent upon wiping the Sioux and every other tribesman from the world. Not content with defeating the warriors, they had continued the slaughter by setting ablaze the tepees in order to force out the old, the women and children. Those who weren't killed fled from the village and those who were caught were either killed outright or used for other sport. She remembered the four who had raped her and left her for dead. She would never forget them, nor would she ever let soldiers touch her again. She would kill them until they killed her.

The authorities had told the tribes that everyone would be protected if they moved on to a reservation. Waktaya didn't believe it; she knew that no court would punish a *wasicun* who attacked anyone from her tribe.

Her hand had settled on the handle of the knife she carried beneath her blanket and her eyes on the sleeping American. He was young and, at the moment, unthreatening, but would she still be safe with him when he recovered from the effect of his wound? She had seen the looks cast in her direction by the soldiers at the reservation and now she didn't trust any of them at all. Not even Jim Braddock, which was why she had been so confused by her grandfather's words.

As he lay in the cave he'd grasped her hand and whispered low so that it had been necessary for her to lower her ear to his lips to hear him.

'He's the one I came to find,' the old man had said, his eyes shifting towards the *wasicun* standing at the mouth of the cave. 'Now, his tepee must be your tepee.' He'd smiled before closing his eyes. Then his breathing ceased and from that moment Waktaya was alone in the world.

Since the death of her father she had honoured no man more than Grey Eagle but her spirit rebelled at his last utterance. True, Jim Braddock had given her no cause for alarm, had helped to raise her grandfather to his resting place, but she didn't want to share his home or his life. When he returned with her pony she would ride away. They would part trails at this point and he could take the wounded man back to his home. But if she were to do that another horse was needed. She had no knowledge of how long their journey would be, but too far, she suspected, for them to ride double. An idea formed in her mind, of a last gesture to write off any debt she might owe the American.

Among her bundle of possessions was a bow and a handful of arrows. She gathered these in her hands, then nudged the sleeping American.

'Your friend will be here soon,' she told him. 'Remain silent. I'm going for your horse.' Before he could form a reply she'd readjusted the blanket around her shoulders and disappeared from sight.

The moonlight was bright and the tracks that had been made on their easterly dash formed a clearly lit pathway back to the cabin.

Although she didn't expect to encounter any horsemen now, she was confident that if any were abroad she would see them long before they spotted her. If not, they would discover her skill with the bow.

Two horses had created enough hoof marks to make it possible for her to place her feet in already broken snow, which speeded the pace at which she was able to cover the ground. After veering on to the higher ground for the last portion of the journey to avoid approaching the cabin from the front, she was soon looking down on the collection of buildings. She paused awhile, surveying the site for movement, watching the smoke rising from the tin spout. This was confirmation that the outlaws were still inside. Satisfied, she began the descent towards the rear buildings.

At the far side of the house, where the privy was situated, the snow had been kicked by a succession of visitors, but the snow that lay between the back of the cabin and the stable was undisturbed. Even though Waktaya's footprints were small, they were, inevitably, clear to see. She had to work quickly and quietly and hope to get away without those inside learning of her visit until it was too late for them to do anything about it.

The horse was at the back of the small stable, almost brushing against the wall of rough wood as though there was additional heat to be gained from it. It was a slim-framed animal, suggestive of the sprightliness that was necessary for a working cow-pony, with a shaggy mane that was two shades darker than its dun coat. It snorted a brief greeting when the girl slipped inside the hut and sidled briskly in the tight space so that it had turned to face her. Waktaya rubbed its muzzle to still and quieten it.

The only light that penetrated the stable's inner blackness came from the partly open door; it took a moment or two for the girl's eyes to adjust to the darkness, which contrasted starkly with the reflected moonlight by which she'd travelled. Setting aside the bow and arrows, she located the necessary equipment, then set about harnessing the horse. The saddle was heavy and throwing it over the beast's back resulted in a series of chinks and slaps as the leather and metal fastenings rattled and slapped in motion.

She paused, listened, and for a moment thought she'd heard the sound of a heavy tread breaking the brittle coating of frosted snow. Her hand grasped the handle of her knife, withdrew it from its soft leather sheath and held it in readiness to strike anyone who entered the stable. She waited, all senses alert for any danger signal. The skin at the back of her neck tingled but there were no more noises, no moving shadows in the doorway, nothing to suggest that her presence had been detected.

Waktaya replaced the knife and finished saddling the horse. Then, after gathering up her bow and arrows, she led the horse outside.

The barrel of a gun was pressed behind her ear and the mechanical sound of its cocking action stopped her in her tracks.

'Figured it was you when I saw the small foot-prints,' Gus Phipps said. 'It was the horse you were after, eh? I thought it was beef you wanted but I suppose horseflesh is just as tasty for you people.'

Waktaya made to move as though there was a pos-sibility of escaping the gunman, but the weapon was pressed more firmly against her head and Gus Phipps laughed.

'You don't really think I'm going to let you get away this time, do you? Drop the bow and arrows,' he told her.

She let them fall and he grabbed her shoulder, his hand filling with the material of the blanket that was wrapped around her. He yanked hard, pulling it away with such force that with a tottering, ungainly movement she was twisted around until she was facing him. Leering, he cast aside the blanket.

'So they send their young 'uns to do their thieving. Well, we know how to punish thieves like you.'

With his left hand Gus Phipps made a grab for the neck of her dress, the intention of ripping it from her body clear to see, but it was a rash action. Secure in the belief that he was in full control of the situation, he had allowed his right hand to drop to his side and the pistol it held was now in a non-threatening position, pointing at the ground.

Waktaya reacted with astonishing speed. In her left hand she still held the reins of Dean Ridgeway's horse and she used them in her defence. She retreated a step, recoiling, it seemed, from the killer's lurch for her dress, but in fact setting herself in a stance advantageous for her retaliation. With maximum leverage in her arms, she launched her attack, swinging the leathers in her hand, once, twice, thrice, striking her assailant's face, aiming for his one good eye.

Gus Phipps yelled, raised his arms in an attempt to protect himself, but to no avail. The lashes cut his face and blood started running freely, so that even when he was able to open his eye his sight was blurred. His natural reaction was to use his gun on the girl, but he never got the chance.

While lashing the leather straps across Gus's face with one hand, Waktaya's other hand gripped the horse's bridle and she ran him forward so that he barged into the outlaw, knocking him to the ground. The pistol flew from Gus's hand and landed several yards away in the snow. Waktaya sprang forward. Now that she was unencumbered by the blanket, her knife was in her hand in an instant. She leapt at the supine figure, aiming to stab him as she landed on top of his chest, but her attack was thwarted.

Gus Phipps had been brawling against tough opponents all his life and he wasn't about to become the victim of a girl. He'd brushed his arm across his face to wipe the blood from his eyes almost as soon as he'd landed in the snow and he'd seen the glint of the blade in the girl's hand. Her leap almost caught him off-guard but he gripped her wrist and twisted it so that the point of the blade didn't pierce his chest. Using the advantage of superior strength he pushed her hand away and began to roll over, intending to get on top to finish the fight.

It didn't prove that easy. Waktaya jutted her head forward and gripped his ear with her teeth. She sank them in and bit until her top teeth ground against the bottom ones. Gus howled, the pain was intense. He flung an open-handed blow at her head, an instinctive response that landed flush on her cheek and knocked her sideways. He twisted her wrist violently; the knife spun away and, freed from its threat, Gus was able to deliver a more substantial blow. Its effect, however, was lessened by the fact that the girl was already moving away from it so that when it landed it was effectually little more than a push that shoved her clear of his body.

Waktaya was fighting for her life and knew that its preservation depended on her reaching the knife or the gun. The knife was nearest and she scrambled through the snow on her knees to reach it. Gus had been just as quick to react and, although he was behind her, he too reached for the knife. It was Waktaya's hand that clamped around the hilt but as it did so the outlaw caught her throat in the crook of his left arm. As he dragged her backwards, his right hand grabbed hers, eventually wresting the knife from her grip. Now in possession of it, he meant to pay her back for the injuries she had inflicted on him. He raised the knife, preparing to plunge it into her heart.

As its arc reached its apogee, his hand was gripped and, in replication of the hold he had on the Sioux girl, someone's arm surrounded his throat in a throttling hold. His hand was twisted, then smashed against a knee, forcing him to release the knife. When it fell into the snow the hold on his neck was released. His first thought was to discover the identity of his new adversary, but as he turned his head to look up a heavy punch landed on the side of his jaw. He sprawled on the ground but his coat was gripped and his head lifted so that another blow could be delivered to his jaw. He grunted and slithered but there was no respite. A third blow crashed into his nose, sending a stream of blood arcing through the air.

Sounds carried from the front of the cabin; those inside had been alerted by the noise outside and were coming to investigate.

Jim Braddock, who had rushed to the cabin when Dean Ridgeway informed him of Waktaya's purpose, hurried the Sioux girl to her feet.

'Quickly,' he urged, 'get on that horse and ride.'

She paused a moment as though about to protest that she wouldn't go without him but she saw his horse waiting at the side of the house. While he ran to his horse, Waktaya sheathed her knife, gathered up her bow and arrows then climbed into the saddle of the other mount. She had almost joined him when the gunfire began.

Drum Hayes had attributed the first outside noises to Gus Phipps returning from the privy, but a moment or two later Choctaw pushed aside the flimsy curtain at the window to peer outside. He thought he'd heard an approaching horse but there was nothing to see. He reported that it was a clear night: no sign of more snow. Then there had been more strange noises and something bumped against the rear wall of the cabin. They'd gone outside to investigate going, out of habit, around the side of the building beyond which stood the privy. That was when they saw the girl riding away, disappearing round the opposite side of the cabin and out of the line of the bullets they fired after her. Choctaw ran to the front of the building, saw that she was accompanied by a second visitor and emptied his gun at them. He wasn't confident he'd hit anyone.

'This time we do it my way,' snarled Gus Phipps, dabbing at the bloody lash marks on his face. 'We find them and we kill them.'

Before they rode away Gus set fire to the cabin.

'Nothing to come back here for,' he declared. 'After I've got my revenge for this,' he pointed at the angry marks on his face, 'we ride on. Besides,' he added, as they watched the rising flames, 'that's easier than digging a grave for Frank.'

TEN

Jim Braddock looked behind and saw the flickering pink glow in the night sky. It was obvious to him that the only thing that could cause such light was the burning of the line cabin.

'They'll come for us this time,' he told Waktaya.

They rode on. Jim was aware that there was a decision to make: whether to follow the tracks they had made earlier or veer away and confuse their hunters by creating a second trail. In the end it was concern for the safety of Dean Ridgeway that forced Jim's hand. They couldn't leave him unprotected and in ignorance of the situation. If they forged a new trail, the chances were that the outlaws would split up and Dean might reveal himself to someone following the original tracks.

The answer, Jim decided, was to repeat the ruse they had attempted earlier. Accordingly, as they neared the place that was Dean's refuge, they slowed their pace to enable Waktaya to pass to Jim the reins of the horse she was riding, then scramble on to high boulders to avoid leaving footsteps in the snow. She did it with reluctance; she had argued against his plan to tackle three killers alone, but Jim had insisted that it was the best way to ensure Dean's safety. In the lad's confused state, Jim told her, the rancher's son was likely to betray his presence to anyone who rode by. The outlaws had already tried to kill him once and perhaps still thought he was dead; they would have no hesitation in finishing the job if they found him again. Unarmed, he would have no chance of survival.

Indeed, in confirmation of Jim's fears, they could see Dean behind the boulders, watching as they approached.

'If I haven't returned by daylight,' Jim told the girl, 'get him back to the site of the cabin. People will be arriving from the ranch who will get him home. Your pony is behind the boulders with Dean so you can begin your own journey home. Be careful.' Then he was gone, leaving Waktaya to join Dean Ridgeway and bring him up to date with the events at the line cabin.

The outlaws were closer behind than Waktaya had expected, the twice-used trail making the going surer for their horses than it had been for those who had created it. But they rode by without any slackening of pace, too intent upon following the tracks that stretched away into the distance to be distracted by the odd disturbance of snow so close to the boulders. Within moments the outlaws were out of sight. Waktaya and Dean were left to wait for events to unfold.

The horse under Jim Braddock was beginning to weary; it had travelled far that day in difficult conditions, sometimes shin deep in drifted snow. He allowed the other horse to draw alongside and, on the run, took his place in its saddle. The more hilly country was being left behind; they were running down the long sloping meadow that led to the tree-lined creek that fed Fetterman's Pool. A glance up at the clear sky showed the Big Dipper in such a position below the North Star as to indicate that almost two hours had passed since midnight. The darkness that was commonly to be expected at this morning hour was offset by the reflection of moonlight, and Jim had no doubt that he presented a stark silhouette against the white landscape. If he was sighted by the chasing gunmen before he reached the trees he would be a sitting target.

The first shot cracked the silence with whiplash sharpness. The bullet struck a tree, scattering snow in all directions. Jim Braddock ducked his head, kicked his heels against the flanks of his mount and dodged into the woodland cover that he'd almost reached without being discovered by the men who were chasing him. He wasn't sure if they had had the opportunity to notice that the second horse was riderless, but now that was of little importance. They had caught him and any thoughts of trying to fool

125

them had to be abandoned. There would be no opportunity to pretend he was riding south, then double-back. He had a fight on his hands and he knew he wasn't favourite to win it.

The fight at the cabin had confirmed for Jim that the men who had killed Harvey Goode and wounded Dean Ridgeway were Frank Felton and his gang. Among his pursuers the patch-eyed face of Gus Phipps was instantly recognizable and Jim knew that punching him into submission had been a mistake. He should have killed him. At the time he'd kidded himself that his reason for not shooting the outlaw was that he'd hoped to get Waktaya away before the other occupants of the cabin became aware of their presence, but that was only an excuse. The truth of the matter was that he wasn't sure he had the courage for a gunfight.

He had killed men during the war but that had been almost twenty years ago. He'd been little more than a youth then, and firing at distant targets was a lot different from shooting a man standing close enough to talk to. It required a ruthlessness such as he doubted he had ever possessed. He didn't know how many men he had to face now, but he was sure they would all be more accustomed than he in the use of a gun and killing people.

Even Waktaya, he thought, had shown a willingness to kill if it was demanded by circumstances. It startled him to find himself thinking of the young Sioux girl and smiling when his life was in jeopardy.

From the cover of the trees he looked back to get

a glimpse of his enemies. He counted three and saw that they were splitting up. One was halfway across the meadow, following the tracks he'd made to the tree line, while the others were riding in wide arcs, one to the left, the other to the right, preparing to catch him between their guns. The immediate choice was to ride on, try to outdistance the gunmen and hope, as he had hoped when he'd attempted the ruse earlier, that they would soon abandon any pursuit that took them towards Big Timber. But that had been in daylight, when there had been a greater chance of alerting the posse. No one would be abroad at this hour.

Jim was also aware of the disadvantage of being chased. As soon as he came within range he would be at their mercy. Without a second thought they would shoot him in the back and leave him to rot where he fell. After that they would wonder about Waktaya. Without doubt Gus Phipps would want revenge. They would backtrack, search more thoroughly for peculiarities in the hoof prints in the snow and they would kill her if they found her. An old Hall single-shot and a bow and arrows wouldn't save her from such vicious men. No, fleeing wasn't the answer. He had to make a stand here and kill them if he could.

He took in his surroundings. He was in a long stand of trees that stretched both ways along the bank of the creek. If he stayed among the trees they were as much an advantage to his attackers as they were to him. They gave him temporary cover but also allowed the outlaws to get close to him unobserved. It didn't need a military tactician to predict that he would soon be overcome in their three-pronged attack. At this place the bank itself rose no more than six feet above the watercourse and so provided a natural breastwork against a frontal attack. However, it gave him no protection on his flanks. Indeed, he would surely be overpowered by any attack along the creek.

Another quick glance in the direction of the pursuers told him he had no more time to deliberate. They were within rifle range and as soon as they saw him they would begin firing. When he moved he almost surprised himself. He pulled his Winchester from its scabbard and dismounted. He slid down the bank, ran across the stream and clambered up the far side. There were trees there, too, and using those for protection gave him a double advantage. His hunters would expect him to remain close to the horses, his leaving them on the other bank would encourage the outlaws to concentrate their search for him around that area. With luck, he would get a clear shot at someone before they realized their error. That could reduce the odds to two to one if he didn't make a mess of the opportunity.

The second advantage to crossing the creek was that his pursuers would be in the open and exposed to his gun whenever they followed. If they didn't plan their attack, came at him one at a time, then he had a chance at survival. He checked the chambers of his revolver, put a cartridge in the empty one, then worked the mechanism of his rifle and waited.

The moonlight that had lit his flight from the cabin was almost obliterated by the trees and it was difficult to discern movement of any kind on the opposite bank. The course of the stream itself was in such dark shadow that it gave the impression of being a long tunnel. But Jim Braddock kept his gaze fixed on the place where he'd left the horses, watching for the smallest movement that would confirm they had not wandered away. He lay still against the bole of a willow, his rifle barrel resting on a raised, snow-covered root, watching, waiting.

A shout first alerted him to the fact that one of the outlaws had found the horses: the one who had followed his tracks, he supposed, because they were the direct route to that place.

'They're on foot!' went up the cry, providing a fillip to the cowboy's spirits. They thought Waktaya was with him, which meant that if they killed him they would continue to search for her in this area. They wouldn't backtrack to find her. She was safe from them and he was content. He took off his hat and rested it, too, on the long root of the willow tree. The night chill was almost painful on his head but he ignored it, he was ready for battle.

No one responded to the call and for three, four minutes, the encircling silence worked on his mind and made him begin to doubt what he'd heard. He was able to pick out the horses but they seemed to be relaxed, not fidgeting, making no sudden movements or giving any of the usual signs that betrayed nervousness. But in the dim light it was hard to be sure. A movement caught his eye, something slight that could have been the flick of a horse's tail or a small fall of snow from a high branch. Jim watched the spot, his gaze fixed, almost staring, so that it was a moment before he realized he was looking at the back of one of the outlaws. The man had dismounted and was moving slowly, carefully, circling around Jim's horses as if he expected to find his quarry squatting at their feet. He was carrying a rifle, it was pressed against his right shoulder ready to be fired.

Jim squinted along his own rifle barrel. A head shot would kill the man outright but it was a smaller target and with the lack of light there was a high risk he would miss. He lowered the barrel, aimed for the man's back and knew that one pull of the trigger would go a long way towards making the confrontation a more even fight. But he paused, shooting a man in the back had such awful connotations. He licked his lips and resighted. His own life was at stake, he reminded himself, and they would shoot him in the back without any qualms.

He held the gun steady, touched the trigger and felt the pressure on his finger, but before he could fire the man moved. He'd turned around, was checking something on the ground. He stepped forward to the edge of the bank and looked down. Suddenly his head jerked up, his eyes became fixed on the far bank: he was looking almost directly at Jim. He had figured it out: their prey was across the stream. He raised his voice to yell his discovery to his partners; that was when Jim pulled the trigger.

The bullet slammed into Choctaw's chest, the force thrusting him gawkily against the horses, his head jagging backwards, his arms flailing for a brief, frantic instant until he hit the ground. The animals shuffled away from the body, sidestepping like affronted spinsters then disregarding it, like veterans for whom the world holds nothing new.

Jim witnessed the effect of his marksmanship through the wisp of smoke rising from the muzzle of his rifle. The success gave him hope but he doubted that the other two outlaws would be such easy targets. In accordance with his pre-set strategy, he rolled to the right. He had decided that remaining in one place would be foolish. Not only would the other outlaws have a location on which to concentrate their attack but it would also soon become apparent to them that they were facing only one gun. He wanted them to believe that Waktaya was still with him. They might be deceived if he kept on the move.

A bullet struck the root of the willow tree, throwing his hat in the air along with a dozen splinters of old, withered wood. One of them stuck in Jim's cheek, slicing like a knife and drawing blood. Even though he was certain that the shooter couldn't see him the cowboy was alarmed by the accuracy of the shot. He figured that the flare from his own rifle must have betrayed his location and had been used as the outlaw's mark. It stressed the calibre of the gunmen he was pitted against. For them, he supposed, hunting men was a natural and enjoyable sport. He was thankful he'd had the notion to move; to do so, it seemed, was now an essential tactic.

Since his fight with Gus Phipps at the cabin Jim had been aware that he was engaged in a kill or be killed situation. Now he knew that it was going to be resolved shortly, here along the creek that led to Fetterman's Pool. Curiously, he found that his mind was working quickly, analysing information and making decisions. He realized that the shot that had been fired had made him aware of that outlaw's position just as his own shot had revealed his whereabouts to his pursuers. Now he had the opportunity to escape the pincer movement by which they'd planned to entrap him.

The shot had come from his left, some distance away on the other side of the creek; that knowledge caused him to stay his movement to the right and adopt a different tactic. It had been his intention to move back among the trees and find a suitable hide. Under cover of darkness he would await an opportunity to kill one of the outlaws, then move to another place to wait for and slay the other. It wasn't much of a plan; it was full of risk and hope, but he was in a situation not of his own making. Years of droving hadn't inspired the military skills of a West Point officer.

Now, however, he saw an opportunity to improve his chances of victory. Having pinpointed the place from which Jim had fired, he figured that the man to his left would still be moving towards that point, getting closer to his target and his partners. So if, unobserved, Jim could get downstream of that man he would have both of the remaining outlaws upstream. By finding cover close to the bank he would have an unobstructed view of the creek and a clear shot at anyone who tried to cross it.

He had been lying in the snow for ten minutes pondering the whereabouts of his enemies. He had expected to hear sounds of horses or harness but nothing had reached his ears. His eyes were aching as he peered through the darkness along the course of the creek, afraid to miss any hint of movement, knowing that any failure on his own part would be fatal. He kept reminding himself that he couldn't afford to show any mercy to his would-be killers; they would have none for him.

Suddenly, before he'd realized that the moving shadows were in fact men, they were almost halfway across the narrow watercourse. He trained his sights on the nearest outlaw and pulled the trigger. There was no yell from the falling figure, it just stumbled sideways and fell heavily into the freezing stream. Jim adjusted the line of fire, searching to pick out the second man, but the outlaw's reaction to the gunfire had been instantaneous. He'd fired two shots in Jim's direction, causing the Broken Arrow rider to abandon his own attack and withdraw further behind the tree he'd chosen for cover. When he looked along the creek again, his quarry was out of sight.

There was no time for regret. Jim had hoped to kill both men while they were open targets; now that he had failed he needed to formulate a new plan. He moved, more quickly now because little more than a hundred yards separated him from his sole adversary. He moved higher up the bank, because holding the high ground was always an advantage, and he used every tree as a hiding-place from which to reconnoitre the way ahead. He was going upstream, towards his opponent, because he guessed the outlaw would expect him to go in the opposite direction. Jim watched for movement, listened for sounds that carried a threat, then moved. Somewhere, he was sure, he would find a suitable niche where he could wait for the appearance of the other man.

A gunshot shattered the silence of the night. A chunk was gouged out of the tree that Jim had just reached, the impact showering him with snow and wood. He moved swiftly, throwing himself forward and rolling downhill, away from the gunman. Jim had been right, the high ground was an advantage, he just hadn't gone high enough. Now he was rolling in the snow and bullets were kicking up the ground all around. One nipped his shoulder but didn't do any serious damage, then he was obscured from the shooter by a thicket of trees and Jim had the opportunity to return fire.

He was on one knee, firing uphill, forcing the outlaw to find his own refuge as the bullets whistled past his head. Knowing he couldn't remain in the open, Jim moved again, scampering downhill, dodging from tree to tree, always endeavouring to keep at least one between himself and the shooter above. In moments he'd reached the bank of the stream and desperately sought suitable cover. He turned and fired three more shots at his adversary then threw himself over a fallen tree. The trunk had fallen over a small boulder leaving a cavity between it and the ground. At the root end of the trunk the space available was like a small cave; Jim pressed himself into it and waited.

The outlaw, when he arrived, was silent and clearly confused by the disappearance of his prey. Not until he stood on the trunk and dislodged a pile of snow did Jim realize that he was close. Suddenly the man jumped down and took three or four steps to the edge of the creek. He reacted like lightning to the sound of Jim behind him, spinning and firing in a fluid, sweeping movement. The shot was an instinctive reaction, going over the top of the fallen tree because he hadn't yet seen Jim. When he did he readjusted his aim towards the corner, but Jim's rifle spoke first. The bullet smashed into the weapon held by Gus Phipps and sent it spinning from his hands.

Jim ejected the spent shell and pulled the trigger once more to end the confrontation. Instead of a deathly explosion there was a hollow, metallic click. He was out of bullets. Gus grinned and reached for his Colt but Jim was not prepared to submit to the outlaw's gun. He launched himself forward, rising from the ground with sudden fury, and drove his head into Gus's midriff. The two men toppled into the stream, each trying to throw a blow that would incapacitate the other. They rolled in the water, first one gaining the upper hand, then the other, but it wasn't until Gus slipped and went down on his back that a winner seemed likely.

Jim stepped forward, grabbed the other by his shirt and pushed his head under the water. He held him down and would have drowned him if Gus hadn't got his hand on a loose rock. He swung it with all his force at Jim's head. Stunned, Jim lay in the river and could only watch as Gus Phipps drew his Colt and prepared to fire.

An arrow passed through Gus's neck. He staggered, eyes bulging and an awful grunt escaped from his mouth. A second arrow hit him in the chest and he fell squirming into the water. He was stilled by a third arrow which thudded into his body, almost touching the previous one.

Jim looked to the far bank where the Sioux girl, back straight and head held high, looked down from her pony.

'Waktaya,' he said. 'The One Who Guards.'

ELEVEN

Charlie Grisham wasn't a man to fret over events. Facing troubles head on had always been his way and he was still around to tell the tales. He'd had a few hard knocks in his time, a few bloody noses, so to speak, but he'd survived the toughest times and nowadays most of his battles were fought with cattle-buyers over a couple of glasses of bourbon. But he was uneasy about the killing of Zeb Walters and more so about the desire of his men to ride up to the high country in search of revenge.

Zeb had been a dependable worker and, in the main, docile in manner, but there had always been an underlying moodiness, a hint of dissatisfaction which had surfaced from time to time. If he had been a different type of man some of those incidents could have led to violence, but most people on the ranch had quickly grasped the fact that Zeb was always more angry with himself than with those with whom he argued. For the crew it was a mysti-fying temperament for a man who, blessed as he was with a wife and daughter, ought to have con-sider himself the luckiest cowboy in the territory.

The rumours regarding Alice Walters and Jim Braddock had reached Charlie Grisham's ears and he couldn't dismiss the possibility that they were true. He'd always thought of Jim Braddock as an estimable man, one to whom he would have will-ingly offered employment at Red Hammer but for the fact that it would have fractured the tenuous friendship between himself and Hec Ridgeway. Jim's high principles and quiet strength would, in Charlie's judgement, make him the sort of man who would attract the attention of women and he could only wonder at Alice's lack of anger when con-fronted with the identity of her husband's killer. Unlike her daughter.

Jane's reaction had been completely different, a circumstance that added greatly to Charlie's misgiv-ings. Despite his arguments Jane had insisted upon being among the group that rode up to Fetterman's Pool, forcing a delay to their departure until the next morning. To make matters worse, Annie, his own daughter, had declared a determination to go along, too.

'I can't let her go alone,' Annie had argued. 'Not only is she my friend but it wouldn't be right for her to be alone among all those men.'

'It's not right for her to be going at all,' Charlie told her. 'Nor you.'

'But go we shall,' his daughter told him.

'Annie,' Charlie had softened his voice, hoping she would listen to reason rather than passion-filled argument, 'the men are talking about a lynching. It's not good to see. It can even sicken tough range riders. I don't want you to see a man die like that.'

'Nor I,' she confessed, 'but I still can't let Jane go alone.'

'Then I guess I'll have to go too. I'll try to persuade Jim Braddock to stand trial. Get him back to Big Timber and hand him over to Ben Stone.'

Annie was grateful for her father's concern; she didn't know how she would react if forced to witness a brutal killing. However, Charlie's reluctance to mete out punishment to Jim Braddock wasn't solely based on the distress it would cause his daughter. He didn't want an outbreak of violence between the Red Hammer and Broken Arrow outfits. The high ground around Fetterman's Pool, like much of the territory around Big Timber, was open range, owned by no man. But the big spreads had grazed their herds on certain sections for years and neighbours had respected each other's predominance in those areas. So, while Hec Ridgeway had no legal claim to the land west of the creek, he was the acknowledged user and any incursion would raise his hackles. If one of his men was snatched from there and lynched, he would want retribution. It could be the start of another range war and Charlie felt too old for that.

139

So, by keeping all his hands at the bunkhouse that night, he hoped to keep word of Zeb Walters's death and the range justice they meant to mete out to Jim Braddock away from the ears of the owner of the Broken Arrow. If Hec Ridgeway didn't learn of the hanging until after the event it wouldn't lessen his anger but it would give him time to reflect on his own response. It might just sway him to the thought that that was the manner in which such matters were handled when there was no lawman around, and that he would have done likewise in similar circumstances. Charlie tried to convince himself that he believed there might be a chance it was true.

Of course, in a small town like Big Timber, word of events spread more quickly than a prairie fire. Alice Walters imparted the plan to Cec Goater when she went along to view her husband's body in the undertaker's parlour. Perhaps her words had been spoken merely as an outpouring of grief but the undertaker had a reputation as the biggest gossip in town, so it was no surprise that he broadcast the details to all and sundry who drank that night in the Garter. Among the customers were a couple of Broken Arrow riders, who hightailed it back to the ranch to inform Hec Ridgeway of the Red Hammer plan.

At dawn a group led by Charlie Grisham, which included his daughter and Jane Walters, rode away from Red Hammer. Their route took them across the Red Hammer range and up to a point just south

140

of Fetterman's Pool where they cut west on to Broken Arrow land. From there it was a five-mile ride to the line cabin, where they hoped to corner Jim Braddock.

Some time later Hec Ridgeway, with a well-armed bunch of Broken Arrow riders, set out with the same destination in mind.

Following the fight in the creek Jim Braddock's clothes were sodden. The water wasn't deep but in his fight for life it had lapped over him, penetrating to his skin. Now, the clothes were hardening with ice and the bristles on his face were white with frost. He shivered, fiercely, and found that he couldn't stop.

Waktaya hurried him on to the bank, made him lean against her pony to get warmth from it while she hustled the other two horses to join the pony in an unusual triangle formation around him. Because he was trembling and virtually unable to help himself, she set to work removing his clothes. Then, dragging the rough, dried-grass blanket from the back of her pony, she wrapped him in it from shoulders to knees. It was dirty, but that detail escaped Jim's attention, as did the scratches it inflicted on his body when Waktaya scrubbed it against him to achieve the double affect of warming him and absorbing the moisture that clung to his skin.

After working at the task for several minutes and assured by the renewed colour of his skin that her

141

efforts had been successful, she went in search of something more permanent in which to clothe him. The bodies of Gus Phipps and Drum Hayes still lay in the water and she left them there. Choctaw Jennings was stretched out on the bank, legs straight and arms flung wide. He wasn't as big as Jim Braddock but, until something better could be found, what he wore would have to suffice. She stripped the dead outlaw and carried his clothes back to Jim. While he dressed, she unsaddled the other horses whose blankets would aid their own warmth.

'There are matches in my saddlebags,' Jim announced. 'I'll find some suitable kindling and we'll get a fire going.'

Wakataya put a hand on his chest. 'The women of the Hunkpapa Sioux know how to gather sticks,' she told him, her voice bearing an inflection that suggested she was affronted by his words, that she was more than capable of carrying out the duties that were hers to perform. She wasn't prepared to forsake the customs of her people to appease any *wasicun*, not even the man for whom she was harbouring a growing liking and admiration.

They sat side by side with their backs against a sycamore tree, wrapped in horse blankets and becoming drowsy with a combination of weariness and warmth from the flames. When they awoke a couple of hours later their heads were touching, hers cushioned against his shoulder and his rested against it. They stirred simultaneously and smiled at each other with awkward pleasure.

It was daylight and the sun promised warmth as though yesterday's snow had been a mistake and wouldn't be allowed to return until its due time. Getting back to Dean Ridgeway became Jim's priority, the ranch owner's son had been left in the high ground without either a horse or a weapon. While Waktaya undertook the task of saddling the horses Jim set about dragging the bodies out of the creek. He didn't intend giving them any sort of burial; he just hauled them on to the bank so that their rotting bodies didn't contaminate the water. He had no doubt that some predator would soon be enjoying a free feed.

He was studying the faces of the three bodies, perplexed by the fact that he didn't recognize any of them as Frank Felton, when an unaccountable sensation caused him to turn his attention to the Sioux girl. He hadn't been alerted by any sudden noise or cry of alarm, Waktaya had been going about her business with the same quiet efficiency that had marked everything she'd done since he'd first met her, but something had changed, something subtle in her silence but as startling as a scream of danger.

Waktaya was still with the horses, perhaps twelve yards away, but moving backwards, getting closer to him, taking small, cautious steps, her weight on her toes as though preparing to flee from a fearful enemy. Her right hand was reaching to her side where her knife was sheathed beneath the draping

143

blanket. Jim was about to break the silence, wanting to know the cause of her worriment, but suddenly the answer became abundantly clear.

All around them, soldiers emerged from the trees, rifles extended, bayonets fixed as though in readiness for a charge. A voice rang out, the command to stand still directed at Jim and Waktaya. The troopers began to advance in a menacing fashion, their formation designed to confine the pair to the bank of the creek. One of the troopers circled around by the horses and approached Waktaya. In contradiction of the shouted command, he gestured with his rifle for her to get away from the animals. His face was white and his eyes were watching the girl fixedly. It was a nervous expression, one that alarmed Jim, suggestive as it was of a man capable of irrational reactions.

'Hey, this one's a squaw,' said the soldier, stretching forward to prod her with the bayonet tip.

'Don't do that,' Jim yelled, hurrying forward, disregarding the threat from the rifles that covered him. His words were directed at the soldier but could just as easily have been meant for Waktaya. From his viewpoint he could see her hand clamped around the handle of her knife; he feared that if she drew it she would be killed.

A command to stand still was given again, but Jim paid it no heed. He reached Waktaya and pushed himself between her and the bayonet, partially hiding her and glaring defiance at the young trooper. He knew that her knife was now

144

unsheathed and gripped in her right hand with firm intent, as though resolute in her determination to defend herself, but her left hand, which was pressed against his back, trembled. She was clearly terrified at the prospect of being in the hands of soldiers and Jim knew she was prepared to die rather than submit to them. His right hand reached behind to find hers in an attempt to hide the knife she held from the eyes of the uniformed men.

'Stand back, Johnson,' a voice commanded the trooper. The man who intervened was older and surprised that he recognized Jim's face. 'You!' he exclaimed.

'Yes, Sergeant. It's me. Who did you think it was?'

'Thought you were Grey Eagle's band. We saw the smoke from your fire then spotted a body with arrows in it lying in the water.' Lieutenant Cooper hurried forward to join them and listened while Jim gave an account of the death of Harvey Goode, the wounding of Dean Ridgeway and the burning of the line cabin.

'They are members of the Frank Felton gang and were intent on killing us too. A posse out of Big Timber is hunting for them.'

From time to time during the telling of the story, Lieutenant Cooper's gaze had lingered suspiciously on the figure of the girl who had remained shielded by Jim's body.

'Who is she?' the officer asked. 'Is she Sioux, one of the renegades?'

Waktaya's reaction to the new arrivals had

removed any lingering thoughts Jim might have had for placing her safe return to Pine Ridge in the hands of the army. She would resist them with every ounce of her being. He wasn't sure which of them would be in more danger of harm from the other: the troop of soldiers or the Sioux woman. What he did know was that he couldn't tell the truth.

'She's my wife,' he announced. Jim found it an easy lie to tell. 'She's always lived in these parts.'

If the lieutenant's face wore an expression of doubt, his sergeant's was one of utter disbelief. The thought crossed Jim's mind that the sergeant had recognized Waktaya, had seen her at Pine Ridge and knew that she was the granddaughter of Grey Eagle, but the moment when it seemed probable that he would give voice to his suspicions passed and further explanation became unnecessary.

'You can return to Pine Ridge,' Jim told them. 'Grey Eagle is dead. He came to die in the Holy Place he knew as a boy.'

'How do you know that?' Again the lieutenant cast a suspicious glance in Waktaya's direction.

'The Sioux are mystical people, Lieutenant. They have their own way of sending messages. The birds, the animals, the trees and the wind speak to them. I don't know how they do it, but their way is as sure as a telegraph message. All the warriors who left with Grey Eagle have returned to Pine Ridge.'

Jim wouldn't disclose the location of Grey Eagle's body but Lieutenant Cooper was reluctant to abandon his mission without absolute proof that the old chief was dead. The sergeant, however, was more versed in the customs and practices of the tribespeople, and he gave voice to the fact that he'd heard similar stories in the past. By the time the soldiers departed his words, bolstered by the advance of winter and a shortage of rations, were beginning to have an effect on the younger officer.

Jim and Waktaya watched them go before climbing on to their own mounts and heading back for the place where they'd left Dean Ridgeway. Despite the need to reach Dean, they rode on in unhurried fashion.

They had climbed into the higher ground when they saw the swiftly moving group below. The group had swung into sight momentarily as it passed a gap in the tree line, then it was gone again as they continued towards the Broken Arrow line cabin. It was a larger group of men than Jim had expected but he had no doubt that they were the men of the Red Hammer crew, who had been sent to collect their injured comrade. Because they would find Harvey Goode's body frozen in the snow, Jim decided it was imperative to join them to explain the situation.

With Dean Ridgeway's horse in tow Waktaya continued on the route that would take her to the ranch owner's son while Jim made a beeline for the burnt-out cabin. Apart from the size of the group that had ridden up from Red Hammer, two other aspects of it troubled him. Their purpose had been to transport home a man with a broken leg but he couldn't recall seeing a wagon, and he'd recognized the palomino that was leading the rescuers. Why was Charlie Grisham bothering himself with a mundane rescue run?

Judd Quaterstaff was the first of the horsemen to dismount and kick at the remains of the burnt-out line cabin. The roof had collapsed but, due to the heavy snow that had piled against the building, the remaining walls were standing, though blackened, irregular shapes.

'Reckon he's ridden on,' Judd announced. 'Probably gone west over the hills and across the border.'

Pat Hunt disagreed, indicating the trodden trail leading east.

'More than one horse made those tracks.'

'Young Ridgeway was up here riding the line with Jim Braddock,' one of the men informed everyone. 'A couple of Broken Arrow riders were joking about it in the Garter, relieved that old man Ridgeway hadn't isolated them with the lad for a lonely month up here.'

Charlie Grisham grunted in an effort to hide his annoyance. The last thing he wanted was for Hec's son to become involved in the hanging party that would be played out if his men caught up with Jim Braddock. Secretly, he hoped that Jim had gone over the hills to Idaho or up north to Canada. If he was beyond the reach of his men it would put an end to the awkward situation that was developing. He was angry with himself for harbouring such a thought; a man ought to be punished for his crimes but if one guilty man remaining free prevented a range war then he would lose no sleep over it. If Jim Braddock killed Zeb Walters punishment would catch up with him sooner or later. Charlie just hoped it was later.

'Boss!' an urgent call came from Pat Hunt, who had wandered away from the group investigating the track that had been forged in the snow.

Charlie Grisham rode his palomino over to the place where Pat had dismounted and was knelt in the snow.

'What is it?'

'It's Harv. Harvey Goode's dead, too.'

Drawn by Pat Hunt's words, the other horsemen followed their boss. The grimace of death on Harvey's face was unpleasant to see. Annie Grisham swiftly turned away from the sight but Jane Walters looked upon the body with an expression that showed little pity. The death of another man that could be attributed to Jim Braddock would harden the resolve of the men to exact punishment. The gossip in the store following her father's night in the cells, echoed once more in her mind but no one would be able to say that young Harvey had been killed because Jim Braddock wanted her mother.

The prospect of those sniggering accusations resurfacing in the wake of her father's death had worried her, but this second killing and the summary justice that would follow would surely deflect any criticism from her mother. A second killing must convince everyone in Big Timber that the root of the trouble was antagonism between the two big outfits.

'Looks like he's been dead some time,' Pat told everyone, pushing snow off the upper torso to demonstrate how long the body must have lain there. 'Why kill Harv?'

Charlie Grisham had dismounted to examine the body of his dead ranch hand. 'What was Harv doing here?' he wanted to know. 'What's been happening?'

'We won't find out until we find Jim Braddock or young Ridgeway,' Pat answered.

Judd Quarterstaff pushed his way through the throng of horses and pointed back to the ruins of the cabin as he spoke to the Red Hammer boss.

'You won't learn anything from Dean Ridgeway. There's another body over there, burned black and unrecognizable, but I guess Braddock's killed the kid, too.'

A silence settled over the group, their anger at the discovery of Harvey Goode's body now muted by the confusion caused by the latest discovery. Some of the Red Hammer riders had found difficulty in attributing the killing of Zeb Walters to Jim Braddock; now, inexplicably, there were two more dead men and a burnt-out cabin to account for. Their musings were interrupted by the muffled thuds of a fast-approaching horse.

Jim Braddock dismounted almost before he'd reined his mount to a halt and hurried to the side of the Red Hammer boss, eager to divulge details of the events that had led to the killing of Harvey Goode. He was aware that his arrival had given rise to several murmurings and he picked up on the mood of anger that they implied, but he attributed it to their discovery of Harvey's body. He certainly wasn't prepared for the accusations and fury that were about to be unleashed.

Charlie Grisham spoke first, unable to keep the rancour from his tone; the discovery of the body that he assumed to be that of Dean Ridgeway had freed him from the fear of Broken Arrow retribution in the wake of a lynching.

'Thought you'd fled,' he said, 'skipped off to Canada to escape the law, but I guess you figured that no one would suspect you of the killings.' The bemused expression that settled on Jim Braddock's face didn't halt Charlie's words. 'Zeb was still alive when he reached the ranch. He named you with his dying breath.'

Jim's surprise at the announcement of Zeb Walters's death was little in comparison to the physical assault that came at him from his left. Jane Walters attacked him with the quirt she carried in her right hand. Its several short leather strips scored lines across his left cheek and neck. He yelled, angered by the stinging cuts. Twisting and bending, he used his left shoulder and arm to ward off the blows.

'You murdered my father,' Jane shouted, continuing to lash out with the riding whip raining blows on him with increasing frenzy.

Jim tried to push her hand away, tried to protect his face from the flicking, snapping thongs. If she continued, the loss of an eye was a distinct possibility. He jabbed out with his left hand, the heel of which connected with Jane's jaw. She wasn't seriously hurt by the blow but it surprised her and the rigidity of his arm caused her to stagger backwards and almost fall. It provided Jim with a moment of respite in which he tried to assemble his thoughts to rebut the charges made against him.

However, the repulsing of the attack from one side only gave rise to another; this one was delivered with the weight and power of a man who was proud of the strength he possessed, a symbol of the toughness he'd needed to survive the rough life he'd lived.

'Not just a back-shooter but an abuser of women, too.' Judd Quarterstaff's words were swiftly followed by his huge right fist crashing against Jim's jaw. Jim went down, tumbling among the legs of men and horses. Judd grabbed his shirt, pulled his upper body clear of the ground then smashed his fist once more into Jim's face.

Consciousness returned slowly, the stings emanating from the quirt-inflicted wounds being the first stimulus to rouse him from his state of senselessness. The full picture, that he was astride his horse with his hands tied behind his back and a thick rough rope fitted tightly around his neck, took him several moments to realize. He was being held upright by two Red Hammer cowboys, men he recognized, with whom he had joked, drunk whiskey and played poker in the Garter. But they weren't smiling now and from behind them, out of Jim's vision, came the voice of an angry woman.

Jane Walters was demanding the right to slap the rump of Jim's horse and send him swinging to hell. Charlie Grisham was resisting her demand, reluctant to have her memories and her reputation tainted by the deed for the rest of her life.

'Boss,' Pat Hunt called and pointed to the south where a bunch of riders were fast approaching.

'What's going on?' Hec Ridgeway demanded to know. 'Get rid of that noose and untie that man.'

Charlie Grisham had moved away from the hanging tree to meet his Broken Arrow counterpart.

'He's killed some men, Hec. Shot Zeb Walters in the back and the body of Harvey Goode is lying over there in the snow.'

'If you think you've got some proof he did it then take it and him to the sheriff in Big Timber. Jim Braddock never killed anybody that didn't need killing.'

'Zeb named Jim Braddock with his last breath,' Charlie said.

'And what does my son say? He's up here with Jim.' Hec looked around at the faces gathered around the condemned man. He scowled at the presence of the girls, it was unseemly, an offence to his principles. He had thought better of Charlie Grisham than to allow them to witness such ugly business. Words to express his displeasure were forming in his head but Charlie was the first to speak.

'I've got bad news for you, Hec. Your boy, he's among the dead. He's over there. His body was in the cabin when it was set afire.'

Hec Ridgeway spurred his horse up to the remains of the cabin, dismounted and sought out the unrecognizable body among the blackened timbers. Charlie Grisham gave him his version of events when, pale-faced, he returned to the group around the tree.

'Reckon he killed your boy first, then burned the cabin down to hide the crime. My boys must have seen the smoke, come over here to investigate and got killed for their trouble. It could only have been Jim Braddock. There's no one else within miles of this place.'

Jim Braddock was trying to get the attention of the Broken Arrow boss, wanting to tell him the truth of the matter, wanting to tell him that he didn't know whose body had burned in the cabin but it wasn't Dean's. He couldn't speak, however, his neck was stretched and the knot was hard against it, making it impossible for him to produce any sound other than a harsh, meaningless gurgle.

Grim-faced, Hec nodded his agreement with Charlie's account of the killings and stepped forward to whip the horse out from under Jim Braddock himself. He lifted his hat from his head and raised it high, prepared to sweep it across the animal's tail so that it would jump forward and leave its rider dangling on the end of the tightening noose. He looked up into Jim's face, bitterness in his eyes and a curse on his tongue.

Annie Grisham regretted joining the group that morning. Her presence had not been a benefit to her friend. Jane's lust for vengeance had made her deaf to advice. Now, Annie sat at the back of the riders, her head bowed, reluctant to witness the death of a man who, whenever they had met in Big Timber, had never shown her anything but gentle respect. Out of the corner of her eye she caught the movement of Hec Ridgeway raising his hat. Startled, and aware that this was the moment of execution she turned away. Her eyes settled on an unexpected sight.

'Stop,' she yelled at the top of her voice and heads turned in her direction. Beyond her, many of the men saw the riders who had caused Annie to put a halt to the lynching.

'That's Dean, Mr Ridgeway,' declared one of his cowboys.

Until he'd confirmed for himself that his son was indeed one of the approaching riders, the old man kept his hat raised in readiness to carry out the hanging, but it took only a moment before he was rushing forward to greet his son. The group shifted its focus away from the condemned man and directed it instead to the reunion between father and son. One or two of the cowboys wondered about the identity of Dean's companion but the immediate concern was to hear how he'd escaped the supposed slaughter meted out by Jim Braddock.

Waktaya arrived at the scene with horror in her eyes. She didn't know why Jim Braddock was under sentence of death, all she knew was that those who were preparing to hang him were in the wrong. She had been reluctant to follow Dean's example and stop outside the ring of cowboys to discuss the matter. The important thing to do was to remove the noose from around Jim's neck.

The reason that Dean Ridgeway was still alive held little interest for Jane Walters. The perceived slights still taunted her and fed her belief that Jim Braddock was responsible for the death of her father. She was determined he must hang for it. While everyone had their backs to the hanging tree she raised her quirt and whipped the horse on which Jim Braddock sat. It sprang forward. leaving him dangling and kicking in the gap between branch and ground.

Waktaya, whose concentration on Jim Braddock had never wavered, saw everything. Kicking against the flanks of her pony, she barged through the assembled throng to reach him. Manoeuvring alongside the writhing figure, and with incomprehensible strength, she held and lifted Jim's body until his weight, like her own, was borne on the back of her pony. A dreadful gasping sound rattled in his throat and his eyes were so tightly closed that it seemed they might never open again. Waktaya drew her knife from its scabbard.

In the moment after reaching Jim Braddock, Jane Walters had been sent sprawling by the darting pony. From her position on the ground she watched Waktaya's single-handed rescue. Now, as the Sioux woman's eyes fixed on her, she was afraid. The knife in Waktaya's hand glinted a warning. Jane was ignorant of Waktaya's name: The One Who Guards, but the look Waktaya shot in her direction was unmistakable: she would kill if anyone tried to harm the man again.

Waktaya didn't use the knife on Jane Walters. Instead, she sliced the ropes that bound Jim Braddock's hands so that he was able to loosen, then remove the noose around his neck. He coughed and spluttered, and rubbed his fingers against the burn marks that had been inflicted by the rough rope. Waktaya held him tightly while Dean Ridgeway told the full story to the gathering; informing them that Gus Phipps had killed Harvey Goode, that it was Frank Felton's body that had been incinerated in the burning line cabin and that the remainder of that gang lay dead on the banks of the creek that formed the boundary line between the grazing ranges.

He didn't have an explanation for Zeb Walters uttering Jim Braddock's name with his final breath but assured everyone that the Red Hammer man should have been halfway to the ranch before Jim set off for the high ground looking for strays. Somewhere along the trail, Dean suggested, Zeb had fallen foul of Frank Fenton and his gang and they were responsible for his death.

'Guess we owe you an apology,' Charlie Grisham said to Jim Braddock.

Jim didn't respond, too angry to know what to say or even if he ever wanted to speak to these people again.

'There'll be a reward for the capture of Frank Felton and the others. You'll be a wealthy cowpoke.'

'Waktaya killed Gus Phipps,' Jim said, the words hurting his throat and sounding like the grating of a blacksmith's rasp against horseshoes. 'That money is hers.'

There was an uncomfortable silence. Everyone knew that reward money wouldn't be paid to a Sioux or to a member of any of the other tribes across the country. Jim knew it too: he just wanted them to feel a little more uncomfortable.

'We'll see to it that you get every cent you deserve.' Dean Ridgeway told him, looking to his father for confirmation.

'Sure, sure,' said Hec. 'When we get back to the ranch. . . .'

'I'm not going back to the ranch,' Jim declared. 'I've been there ten years and I saw today how much my loyalty is worth to you. Didn't even give me the chance to tell my story, Mr Ridgeway. You'd have swatted the horse out from under me and never given the matter another thought.'

'I thought you'd killed my son,' Hec Ridgeway said.

'But I hadn't. So you go your way and I'll ride on with the only person I can trust.'

There were no goodbyes. The Red Hammer riders were the first to leave, Charlie Grisham leading the way on his palomino, cutting an easterly trail that would take them south of Fetterman's Pool and on to their own range land. A chastened Hec Ridgeway went south, leading the Broken Arrow crew, men with whom Jim had worked but who parted from him like strangers. Only young Dean Ridgeway, his head swathed in a fresh bandage, raised a hand as he passed the place where Jim and Waktaya stood.

'I've decided,' Jim said, picking his words with caution, unsure how the fiery Sioux woman would react to what he proposed, 'that when you go back to Pine Ridge I'll go with you. It'll be safer that way.'

'And if I choose not to return to the reservation?'

Jim looked at her questioningly. He wasn't sure where else she could go but a kind of serenity had settled on the girl and he was loath to destroy it. Even though he had no clear idea of what the future held for him he was aware that his life and Waktaya's were now inextricably linked.

'Then I'll take you wherever you feel most safe. Where you go, I'll go.'

The doubt she had once had for her grandfather's final words had long since disappeared. When Jim Braddock had pushed himself between her and the soldier's bayonet point, she had known that her future home would be with him.

'I feel safe with you,' she said. 'Where you stay, I will stay.'